THE E.N.D'S TALE

BOOK 2

LUNA'S BONDS OF LOVE

MICHELLE GODFREY

Copyright © 2023 Michelle Godfrey
All rights reserved.
ISBN: 978-1-960759-03-0

SPECIAL THANKS

Thank you to my family for pushing me towards my goals. Without your support I would never have made it this far.

CONTENTS

The Prism Prison. The fierce, dark, shapeshifting cube that holds the top worst criminals. Here remains Aaron forever locked away in his cell. He would often think of his wife Luna and son Aaron Jr. His son would visit him often but hadn't seen Luna in quite some time. She stopped visiting once she slipped him the key after her final visit. Aaron knew it must have been painful to see him locked away like that. He vowed that he would return to her again. Thinking of his family made him remember his own in the past. He often thinks about his childhood growing up.

Thinking of his childhood made him wonder what kind of man he would have been if he still had his parents. Like Queen Eve, Aaron's mother, born a Royal, married his father a common born. She was eventually discovered and taken by the royal guards to marry her king. He was only a young boy when his mother was taken. Aaron grown bitter and was filled with hatred about the rules of these worlds. His father passed away due to the heartbreak of losing his wife. Aaron's life changed dramatically which led to his life as an assassin.

As Aaron continued to drift to and from his memories of the past, listening and studying the guards was still his top priority. Aaron would listen as the guards made their rounds every day. The guards would walk the halls speaking ill of the ones who reside in the prison. He listens as two of the guards stopped in front of his cell to conversate.

"Hey, hey Jake! Over here!"

"Yeah, what is it Jason?"

"That August guy is getting release today, isn't he?"

"Yeah, lucky bastard. If he wasn't friends with the Queen, he'd be dead already."

"In my opinion I think we should kill him anyway. He nearly got us all killed."

"We have our orders, Jason. We are to release the bastard. It's that Aaron guy who will never see the night sky again."

"Yeah, now there's a guy who should be dead."

Aaron was annoyed listening to the guards have this conversation nearly every day about him. The guards continue to talk about him in a foul manner. Aaron let out a sigh.

"I won't be here long." he says under his breath. "Luna left me this key for a reason. I shall not waste it. Now isn't the right time to escape though. I must be patient a little while longer. I will see you again, my beloved wife, Luna. For now, I will rest and save my strength. I'm going to need it."

CHAPTER 1

NEW PLANS NEW LIFE

The next day Luna walks through the streets of what used to be a small village. She investigates her home where she and her friends used to live and play. Seeing how much had changed was exciting for her but also brought upon sadness. Her best friends were not around anymore. Now, there were plenty of new families that had arrived to live in the place they called home. The village has grown into a massive Kingdom full of buildings and gardens. Luna smiles at the people as she walks the streets. They remember the day she delivered the message for their lives to be saved. Eve's plan to save the people had paid off. The people were always welcoming and kind.

"I'm going to miss this place. I have so many memories here. Some are good, and some are sad. Either way, this place was my home where I met my friends and foster family. Not to mention, I met Aaron on this world. He was the beginning of how my life came to be. I truly miss him and hope to see him again. My love for him is forever, we are bonded. I just hope he feels the same way about me whenever he is free. I might just be optimistic about the whole idea, but I believe he will return to me once again. Heck, he doesn't even know that I have given birth to two more children, not his own. Maybe I should stop overthinking things."

"Luna! Luna"

"Oh, Mr. and Mrs. Madison. It's good to see you again."

Mrs. Madison reaches for Luna's hand and holds it firmly. She rubs her belly and smiles. "Luna, because of your brave action, I can finally have a child and live to raise them."

"No, no, it was nothing really. Queen Eve was the one who sent me on that journey."

"Ha ha, don't be so modest Luna." Mr. Madison says, "We thank you and the Queen for such kindness. No one has ever gone journeying into those woods alone just to save others. You saved my wife and unborn child. I am forever grateful. It seems the other platforms had taken notice of what you and the Queen have done. The other Kings and Queens are starting to follow our Queens lead. This is history in the making where the lives are being saved around the skies."

"Oh my, thank you for your words, Mr. Madison. I never really thought of the changes in that way. My sis Eve always wanted to change the worlds. I see its finally happening."

"Well, it has changed. Now me and my husband won't keep you any longer. We just had to thank you after seeing you again."

Luna gives a shy smile and waves them goodbye. She continues to make her way to her old home and opens her door. She exhales when she steps inside. The Madisons weren't the only ones who saw Luna and Eve as heroes. Luna didn't feel that way since she knew August never meant to hurt anyone. Thinking of August made her realize that the mistake he made was because of how much he cared for her and Eve. She hates how the people see him as a traitor or someone who would purposely cause harm to the people. That was another reason she had to leave.

"I still have more packing to do. It's not much though. Leaving this world seems strange but it's for the best. Eve has a new life and responsibility to her Kingdom. Not to mention she is raising new kings and queens."

While Luna was thinking she heard the front door open. Luna stops her packing and looks over with excitement.

"Miquel! You're home!"

Luna heart melts every time she sees Miquel. She runs over to him as he was her second husband and love of her life.

CHAPTER 2

LUNA'S 2ND HUSBAND

Miquel walks over to Luna and grabs her by the waist and kisses her passionately. Luna moans as he pushes her up against the wall and continues to kiss her. Luna was becoming horny by his actions but pulled herself together.

"My love I thought you had to work late tonight?"

"I was supposed to work late tonight Luna, but the Queen gave me permission to leave early. I can help you with packing our things to move. Moving to a new platform is hard work you know."

"Hm, it's just like Eve to be so kind to me. Even after everything that's happened, she still looks out for me. She takes very good care of our children in the Palace. I love her and the whole family."

"Well, she is like a sister to you. If I didn't know your story, I would have thought you were blood related."

"I know right. So how are our kids doing? I've been so busy packing these last few days I haven't had a chance to see them."

"They are doing well, enjoying the Palace life. You know the Queen loves the fact that you keep birthing Royal born children. Her daughters will have plenty of Kings to marry in the future. Plus, it still amazes me that you are a Noble born Luna. They are just as rare as Royals if not rarer. This is a key reason you keep having so many Royal born children."

"Well, you were the one to discover that after I kept having so many Royal babies. I never would have imagined that I was special. Well, it doesn't matter, I will give birth to all the royals she needs. It brings me joy being a part of this family and how big it has become."

"So do I, my love."

"Miquel, you know... I've been thinking about Aaron. One day he will see your symbol of bonding love on my back. How would I explain?"

Miquel gently lifts Luna's chin and looks her in the eyes. He plants a kiss upon her soft lips. "Luna, my love, we will worry about that when the time comes. I will be with you when we explain to him. I know Aaron, he will be fine."

"How could you be so sure? I understand that you know him but… never mind. I'll just have to trust your judgment. You seem to always be right for some odd reason."

Miquel let out a chuckle. "I'm not always right. I just do my best at analyzing the situation, that's all. But on to other matters, I was wondering if you had successfully slipped Aaron the key?"

"I did. I hope it helps him in some way."

"Don't worry, it's good that he has the key. Give Aaron some time. He is not going to rush. He will be at the other platform sooner than we know it."

"Your confidence gives me reinsurance. I feel better now that I've talked to you."

Miquel smiles and kiss Luna on the forehead. "Now, let's continue to pack. Well, that is after I'm done with you of course."

Luna bit down on her lip as she stares at her husband's lean muscle tone body. She let out a sharp breath before she spoke.

"What do you mean?" she asks looking down at his already hard penis.

"I mean, I wouldn't mind having you before we leave Luna."

"O-ok, just try not to get me pregnant alright. Eve goes crazy every time I bring another royal baby her way."

Miquel laughs at her statement. "You are right she does love our sons. They will make fine Kings one day. We will visit them before we leave."

"I would love that."

"Now enough talk, I need you now Luna."

Miquel pulls Luna close so that he may kiss her while grabbing on to her nice round ass. He gave it a hard squeeze as he bites and sucks on

Luna's neck. Luna moans as her husband plays and teases her body. He knew every spot to make her body twitch and tremble. Luna slowly unbuttons his pants and strokes his hard penis. He let out a moan from her firm strokes. Their breathing intensifies as they continue to please one another. Miquel unzips the back of Luna's moon dress and lets it fall off her perfect hourglass figure. Miquel moves down to lick and squeeze on her large breast as she strokes her figures through his long flowing white hair. Luna moans and breathes heavily as he continues to lick down her body.

"Hah. Miquel, you always know how to play with my body. Your tongue is hitting all the right spots."

Miquel knew how to drive his wife crazy. He walks her over to the couch and lays her on her back. He took his time sliding her panties down her thick thighs. Luna's legs began to tremble before Miquel could eat her pussy. He knew he had control over her mind and body. A smile comes across his face as he watches his wife squirm nervously. Miquel lowers his face between her legs and kisses her thighs down to her pussy. Luna's eyes roll and her legs shake uncontrollably.

"Ah, yes Miquel. I love you! You're amazing!"

Luna plays in his hair as he grips her thighs tighter forcing his tongue deeper inside of her.

Miquel loves how she tries to run from him. Her body couldn't handle much more of the pleasure he was giving her.

She whispers softly. "Hah, Miquel. I can feel myself..."

"Oh, I know. I can taste all of it."

Miquel smiles at her as he rises to his feet. "I'm just getting started my dear. But for now, it's your turn."

Miquel pulls Luna forward and places his penis in her mouth. He let out a satisfying moan as she rolls her tongue around the tip of his penis. Luna watches his eyes roll as she continues to suck and slurp him. Miquel strokes her hair as he pushes a little deeper in her mouth.

"Hah Luna I love how you suck me. This feels so good."

Luna enjoys hearing him being pleased by her. It gave her great satisfaction. Miquel pulls away and lays Luna back onto the couch. He climbs on top of her and slides his rock-solid penis inside her. They let out a moan as he enters her. Luna holds him tight as he slowly starts to stroke deep inside her. His slow-motion vibrates Luna's legs. Miquel leans in and kisses Luna. Their tongues twist and play as he continues. She wraps her legs tight around his body as he strokes faster.

"Ah, ah! Yes! Yes!"

"Hah Luna, I want to hear you beg for more."

"I want more! More Miquel!"

Miquel flips Luna over to her hands and knees. He slides inside her once more gripping the back of her neck. He begins to pound her harder and harder from the back. Luna's moans were so loud the neighbors could hear.

"Tell me who owns you!"

"You own me, Miquel!"

Luna screams as he pounds her harder and spanks her ass. She feels the throbbing of his penis as he releases his warmness inside of her. Miquel pulls her head back by her hair and kisses her lips.

"I love you, Luna."

"I love you too, Miquel."

Luna lays back onto the couch. Miquel pulls out of her wetness fully satisfied.

"Well, I guess we can finish packing now right Luna. Luna?"

Miquel looks down seeing that Luna was fast asleep.

"Or maybe not." He said with a chuckle. "It's fine. I have something very important that I must do before we leave. See you when I get back, my love."

CHAPTER 3

AUGUST FREEDOM

Days passed and August was still locked away in his cell waiting to be released. He wondered if they had forgotten about him and if he would ever see Luna again. He wanted to make matters right with her, giving them a fresh start. August hoped she had forgiven him for his foolish decision he made in the past. Looking back, he knew he messed up the moment he didn't journey with Luna. The assassin situation could have been avoided and Luna would have given birth to his child instead. August remembered the last time they had spoken with one another. Luna had stated she would leave their platform and move to Eve's mother's platform. August sits thinking about Luna and her decision.

"I wonder if she is actually going to live isolated in the forest over there. She hates the creatures of this world. Why would she put herself in danger with unknown creatures on another platform? Could it be that over there the creatures are peaceful. There're platforms that have kind creatures living on them. Maybe that's it. Well, what I'm thinking doesn't matter. What matters is that I get back to her and make things right. I'm willing to accept being husband number two. Heck, that assassin guy is never getting out of here so I will basically be her only husband. I have nothing to worry about."

As August was thinking, he hears a clicking noise at the cell door. It was one of the guards.

"August! You are free to go. Follow me to the exit."

August eyes widen with surprise. Today was the day he was finally free. He'd been locked away for so long his stomach begin to twist and tighten from nervousness. his mind begins to wonder if he even had a home to go back to.

"What were the lands like after so many years have passed?"

August remembers before he turned himself in eleven years ago, he had buried his money and special belongings in the Illusion Woods. Even if he thought his life would end August believed in his heart that there may be a slim chance of his survival. Eve was his childhood friend and family. Their relationship was a little rocky since August did hire an assassin to murder her husband. He knew, since his life was spared, Eve still thought of him as family even after all the trouble and pain he caused her. The thought brought a smile to his face.

"Eve truly is a kind person. She inspires me to make better decisions next time. I never want to cause harm to her or Luna again."

August follows the guard down the hall of the shifting floors and hallways. He wonders how in the world the guards even navigating such a puzzle of a building. Every corner of the floors and walls would move and flash between the colors of purple, blue, and red. A little more navigating through the twisted floors of the prism prison, August finally sees the exit. He whispers to himself as he continues to walk.

"This is really happening. I will finally get to see Luna."

When August exits the prison, he notices immediately Eve waiting outside for him. Seeing Eve filled him with happiness.

"Eve!"

He runs over to hug her when he comes to a sudden stop after noticing the king and Garret standing beside her. August hesitates as he looks at Maximillian.

"You may hug her August." Max says in his usual charming voice. "Just don't get too friendly or I may have to kill you on the day of your freedom."

Max's eyes glow as he grins showing off his sharp fangs. He was clearly toying with August just to watch him tremble in fear. Eve let out a giggle as she watches Max.

"Max, that's enough. You are terrifying my friend."

"Oh, but I was having so much fun."

Max wraps his strong arms around Eve's waist and pulls her close. He kisses her aggressively making her moan slightly.

"Max, not in front of everyone."

"What, we haven't had sex in almost an hour. Can you blame me for being a little horny."

"Max, control yourself." she whispers.

Eve was also feeling the same as Max but was trying not to make it obvious. She starts to walk towards August when she felt Max slap her on the ass. She looks back and gives a shy smile as she blushes.

"You are so going to pay tonight Max." she says in a more seductive tone.

"Oh, I hope so my dear."

Eve continues her walk towards August and embraces him.

August was a little nervous speaking to Eve.

"Well, I see you and your husband are quite naughty even in public."

"Yes, you could say we are. We do have many children due to our affection for one another. I'm so madly in love with him."

"And I almost stole that happiness from you."

"August, yeah you were an idiot, but a lot of wonderful things occurred after your dumb decision. Trust me, you'll see the changes that's been made. Now, on to more positive matters, what are you going to do now that you are free? I need you to stay out of trouble. You're not going to get a second chance you know."

"I know, I've definitely learned my lesson. My plans are to go see Luna and hope to make things right with her."

"Oh August, that's great! But you do know that Luna doesn't live on this platform anymore."

"I know Eve. I was fortunate enough to see her while I was locked away. She told me she was moving to your mother's platform. I'm going to move there as well in hopes to be with her. This might come as a surprise to you, but Luna is ok with me being her second husband. With the assassin locked away it's all good."

"Well, if that's the case, then safe travels on your move and journey to Luna. Make sure you be safe okay. Don't forget to come back and visit sometime. Things can be a bit lonely without you two."

"I will come back, Eve. I will be heading out now. I have to grab my things and hurry off to see her."

"Sure, be careful and farewell."

Eve watches as August hops in the wagon and fades into the distant blizzard. "Wait a minute. Did August say second husband? Does he not know that Luna already has a second husband. Oh boy, this should be interesting."

CHAPTER 4

AUGUST DEPARTS

August finally makes his way into the kingdom that was once a small village.

"Wow, this place changed dramatically. I can hardly recognize anything."

The wagon which August was riding in stops at the front of his old home. August steps out without a single word to say. He stands there with shock at the image of his home. It had been burned to the ground with signs in front. The signs had the words, "scum" and "traitor" written on them. He notices more writing when suddenly out of nowhere a stone is thrown at him. He looks to see the people of his old village and some new faces. They remember what he had done to almost cause them their lives. More of the kingdom's people start to gather around August. A man shouts at him from the crowd.

"That's the man who hired the assassin!"

The crowd begins to rage and shout at August presence. Rocks were being thrown as the people's rage escalated.

"You don't belong here! We could have died because of you!"

August shields himself as he runs through the angry crowd into the woods. His face dripped with blood and his body bruised by the stones. He stares at the kingdom from the distant woods.

"I want to be angry at them, but I can't. They have every reason to hate someone like me. I almost got everyone on this platform killed. People's loved ones, their children, mothers, fathers, everyone. All because I was selfish. I just wanted my friends back and for our lives to be normal. I was willing to sacrifice it all just because I couldn't get my way. I acted stupid back then. Doesn't matter if I leave this place now. I'm no longer welcome here. I guess that makes it easier for me to move on."

August makes his way through the woods to find the location where he buried his belongings.

"I hope it's still here. Yes! My bag, it's still here, my money and clothes, everything. Now I can get out of here and go see Luna. She showed me the location where she will be staying."

August journeys through the woods to cube warp to Eve's mother's platform. The cube was coming into sight. August sprints to the cube and places his belongings inside. He set the coordinates to Eve's mother's location and sits back in his seat. The journey was long and tiring for August, but he finally arrives. He steps out and grabs one of the maps on the stand for newcomers. Looking at the map, August eyes widens and his jaw drops.

"This is Eve's mother's platform?! I've never seen a platform as humongous as this one before. The map itself is complicated to look at. Eve's mother has been Queen a long time now. I'm not surprised that her world would look like this. She must be incredibly powerful. Well, I'm going to study this map a bit. According to the map Luna gave me, it shows that she lives all the way on the other side of the platform in dense forest. Why would she choose such a location? On the world map they don't even have information on this location. It's going to take me weeks if not longer to make this journey. I'm going to need a temporary home to rest before I can take on these lands."

August makes his way towards the kingdom of the platform. He stumbles across a man selling temporary homes for newcomers. Nervously, he walks up to the stand and begins to speak to the person behind the stand.

"H-Hi, I'm new here."

"We have opening on street 649. That will be 30 gold coins." The man says in a monotone voice behind the stand.

The man had to the shoulder length dark blue hair which covered most of the front of his face. He wasn't making any eye contact with August. The man sat boredly, reading his novel while eating berries.

"I'll take the house."

The man hands August the keys and a layout of the home locations. He still didn't acknowledge August presence as he took the 30 gold coins. He exhales and in a non-enthusiastic way he speaks.

"Congratulations on your temporary home."

"Thanks."

August walks away and turns back to look at the man who act as if nothing ever happened.

"What an asshole. He didn't even look my way. (Sigh) It's fine, I won't be seeing him again once I rest up and make my way towards Luna."

August walks the streets until he finds street 649.

"Ah, here it is. Home 385. Let's take a look inside and see how good it is."

The house was already furnished with a table for eating, a couch in the living room, and a master bed in the bedroom for sleeping. The floors and walls where well polish and clean.

"Wow. This is really nice for a temporary home. I think I'll take a shower and hot bath before I eat and rest. Tomorrow will be a long journey. I will be camping in the forest after today. I might as well enjoy it while I can."

After a shower and a long hot bath, August eats a warm meal and lays down to rest. He hasn't felt a soft cozy bed in years. He had forgotten how relaxing it felt to him. He shut his eyes and rested until the morning.

After a long night's rest, August wakes to a hot shower and warm breakfast to start off his day. He packs the things he needs and sets off into the morning night. After journeying for a few hours, August finally reaches the entrance to his destination.

"Well, there's the forest. Luna, I'm on my way."

CHAPTER 5

THE PAST OF AARON

Back on the other platform in the prism prison Aaron sat patiently on his bed. He was preparing his own journey back to Luna as well. The Guards continue to gossip about him as he sits on his bed watching them closely. His patience grew thin seeing each day their routines never change. Tired of watching the guards, he lays his head against the wall and shuts his eyes. Aaron breathes slowly and shuts off his surroundings. It was something he did often to relieve his stress. His mind wonders off to how his life was growing up. Every decision he made led him to his path today. He thought back to his childhood like it was yesterday. The memory of living with his parents was clear in his mind. Melanie his mother, a beautiful Royal born woman. Derrick his father a common born man who tended to their farm. Their faces were clear as day in his mind.

Long ago when Aaron was a child, lived peacefully with his parents on a large farm not far from their village. He was happy living with such a kind gentle mother and his overly protective father. They lived secretly away from the people.

Only one visitor would visit their home selling goods from the marketplace.

"Father. Why do you trust this man? What if he tells mother's secret?"

"I trust him, Aaron. He was a great childhood friend to me growing up. We've always taken care of each other. All this time he still hasn't told anyone of our secret. We need him for the goods that he provides for our farm."

"Well, I don't trust him. I trust no one."

Aaron's mother laughs. "Aaron dear, you must learn to trust others. One day you will need to rely on someone."

Aaron pouts and crosses his arms. "Well, maybe you're right. I still don't trust that guy though."

After grabbing their supplies from Derrick's old friend, they began preparing their afternoon meal. They were sitting together to have dinner when a guardsman burst through the front door.

"See, I told you there was a Royal Queen living here."

Derrick looks over at the door with a shocked expression. He becomes infuriated with the sight. "What is the meaning of this Johnson!? I trusted you! Why would you betray my family?"

Johnson was secretly jealous of Derricks love with Melanie. He felt if he couldn't have her then only the King should.

"You knew the rules, Derrick. Royals belong with Royals. It's not fair that a low life like you have a Queen all for himself."

The guards wrestle with Derrick until they pinned him to the floor. The guard were about to stab him when Melanie steps forward.

"I will go with you! Just leave my family in peace or I'll burn every last one of you to ashes!"

The room was silent in her presence. Everyone knew the power of the Queens.

Aaron's tears were flowing down his cheeks. "Mother, please don't go!"

Aaron's mother embraces him. She gives a gentle kiss on his forehead. "Be brave little one. I must leave you for now. When I am acknowledged as Queen of this platform that's when I will send the guards to retrieve you. We will be together again."

Melanie walks over to Derrick and kisses him one last time. "Goodbye my love. Please forget about me and live. That is the most important thing for you to do."

"No Melanie! I need you. I love you. I will die without you in my arms every day."

The tears raced down each of their faces as it was time for Melanie to be taken. Aaron and Derrick watch as the new Queen was taken away. Johnson was making his way to the wagon when suddenly a sword burst through the front of his chest. He slowly turns to see Aaron with tears in his eyes and a frown upon his face. His eyes were bloody red with a murderous look in them.

"You homewrecker! You destroyed my family, my home!"

Aaron weeps as the man falls dead to the ground.

"Aaron no! What have you done child? He wasn't worth it."

"I don't care father! Mom's gone and you'll die soon. I'll be alone. I don't want to lose you father!"

"Aaron, look at me! I will always be in your heart. I love you. I raised a strong son. Don't let anyone see you in this vulnerable state."

Derrick holds Aaron close to his heart. He kisses him on the head trying to comfort him. Derrick and Aaron didn't notice that they were being watched from the dark trees the whole time of their events. They were busy trying to bury the body, leaving no evidence.

Many months had gone by, and Aaron's father eventually passed away. He lived for as long as he could for Aaron, but his heart couldn't bear the pain any longer. Aaron had been living on his own remembering what his father taught him. He grew his own crops and made his own clothes. Aaron had run low on supplies and had no choice but to head into the village. That early night he went to the village. As he enters, he sees a young red-headed boy being yelled at and called a freak for his appearance. They threw rocks at him causing his head to bleed. Aaron rushes over and catches one of the rocks being thrown. He throws it back, hitting one of the villagers with great force. The villagers took a step back as Aaron had drawn his weapon which was a pair of daggers.

"Anyone else want to throw rocks! You're all a bunch of cowards picking on someone younger than you!"

The villagers whisper how they recognize that he was the Queens hidden child. They walk away not wanting to cause any further trouble to draw out the Queen. One of the men from the crowd turns and shouts.

"That freakish boy doesn't belong here!"

Aaron ignores the idiot man. He looks back to see the red head boy smiling at him.

"Hey, are you alright?"

"Yeah, thanks for standing up for me. No one's ever done that before."

"No problem, my name's Aaron what's yours?"

"Name's Cortez, nice to meet you." He says cheerfully.

"Hey, you should get back to your parents. Your head is bleeding badly."

Cortez let out a laugh. "Parents. What parents. I don't know my real parents and the ones I was staying with abandoned me. I've been living off the land and stealing what I need to survive. My life is harder all due to me being born a little different as you can see. No one wants me around."

"That's horrible Cortez. Your life must suck. Plus, I don't see anything wrong with you. I think your red hair is cool."

"Wow, Thanks! You are the first to say such kind words to me. Want to be my friend?"

"How about brothers? I don't have any family either. I live alone on my farm. I can use a new family if you don't mind."

Before Aaron could finish inviting Cortez, he was being squeezed by him.

"I accept your offer bro."

CHAPTER 6

A BOND FOR LIFE

Aaron and Cortez grew to know one another. Now in their teen years the two boys begin teaching themselves how to fight and defend themselves. They promise to protect and look after one another from the cruel people of the lands. Not long ago the boys decided to move from the farm to a more secluded area. They felt more at peace starting their new lives as brothers. Aaron would never have known that after relocating he would miss his chance at being reunited with his mother. She had sent the Royal guards to retrieve him but was too late. Aaron and Cortez had moved a week before they could arrive.

Now, settling down in their new location, Cortez would often scout the area for new herbs and plants. He happens to stumble across an abandoned village. Cortez notifies Aaron so they can check out the empty village.

"This place was raided by the guards Cortez. The rules of these worlds are cruel. Why do they even exist?"

The two of them walk the village when they hear a girl's scream. Aaron and Cortez ran over to see a young lady about to be taken advantage of by two men. Aaron was disgusted by the sight.

"Hey, leave her alone!"

One of the men turn to look at Aaron. "Who is this bastard? I thought this place was abandoned."

The other man pulls out his weapon. "Looks like we have to take care of these guys so we can play with our new toy."

"These scums. I don't like guys like them Aaron."

"Don't let your guard down Cortez. We must never underestimate our enemies."

The men rush Aaron and Cortez swinging their swords wildly. Aaron dodges and easily catches the man's hand and kicks him in the knees. He snaps the man's leg causing excruciating pain. Noticing the man was caught off guard he quickly slices his throat. Cortez on the opposite side was dodging and rolling out of the bandit's attacks. They cross blades when the bandit attacked until Cortez spots an opening to strike him. After finding his opening, Cortez lunges his sword through the man's heart.

"Well, that was easy. Looks like our training paid off, right Aaron?"

"Yeah, but I still hate guys like them. We need to get stronger just in case we run into more like them."

From the spot the lady was standing a rock was thrown at Cortez hitting him in the face.

They both looked over to her wondering what the heck was her problem.

"What a freak. Why are you here. How could someone that looks like you even exist?"

"You whore! We just saved you and you have the nerve to treat us this way! That's my brother you just hit."

The lady had a small dagger on her side that she grabbed from the dead man's body.

"Don't come near me or I'll kill you both."

Aaron frowns and draws his weapon. "Oh, you can try bitch."

From the roof of the building an arrow flew. It struck the lady straight through the chest. They watch as the lady falls dead to the ground. Cortez and Aaron ready their weapon to prepare to fight again. Two men jumps from the roof and lands in front of them. Their faces were covered by the brown cloaks they wore. Cortez and Aaron can see the long flowing white hair hanging out from the front of their hoods.

"We've been watching the both of you for a while now." The man on the right says.

"You both have the potential of being our apprentices." The man on the left says.

Aaron was on the defense. "We don't trust you! Or anyone but each other!"

"Oh, I like that one." The man on the left says. "I shall train him."

Cortez jumps and raises his hand cheerfully. "Hey, if you are willing to train someone like me then I'll join whatever you're doing."

"Oh goodness, I guess I'll take the happy one." The man on the right says.

"Cortez, we don't even know these guys. They could be bad guys for all we know."

"Oh right, sorry Aaron. Um sorry guys, we don't talk to strangers."

Cortez gives Aaron a wink and a thumbs up. Aaron rolls his eyes at his friend. He knew how naive and goofy Cortez could be. Aaron tries to hold in his laugh at a moment of such seriousness. Meanwhile the two men were talking among themselves.

"You sure you don't want to trade?" The man on the right asks.

"Nope, the red heads all yours. Good luck."

"Fine, I'll show you that my little red head apprentice is better. Now, listen both of you, we are the leaders of the Shadow Stalkers Assassins clan. We have watched over you for some time and would like to personally train and take care of you."

Both men speak in unison. "Will you trust us?"

Aaron and Cortez look at each other speaking without words.

"Will we be safe among your people? If anyone tries to hurt my brother Cortez or treat him differently, I won't hesitate to kill them."

"Oh, I am really excited to train him." The man on the left says. "He reminds me of myself."

"You both will be safe." The man on the right states. "There will be food, shelter, and clothes for you both. Not only that, the both of you will be paid well for your work. What do you say? Will you trust us and come join our clan?"

Aaron shrugs his shoulders. "Fine, I'll join."

"I'll join too! This is so exciting!"

The men speak in unison once more. "Excellent choice."

"Now, let's make way to our new home." The man on the left stated.

CHAPTER 7

THE SET UP

Many years had passed since Aaron and Cortez joined the assassin's clan. They were trained to be the very best compared to the other clan members. Aaron and Cortez still couldn't defeat either one of their leaders in mock combat training making them the second best of the clan. The men have been on hundreds of successful missions which made their senses sharp and their body stronger than ever. Before their next mission they would sit and chat to relax their minds.

"So, Aaron, what's your mission this time?"

"I have been summoned to do a job for someone. They ask for me specifically."

Cortez gives Aaron a worrying expression. "Um, that sounds a bit weird to me. Be careful bro, no one is supposed to know our names to begin with. I usually don't have bad feelings about things unless it's serious. So, watch your back ok. You don't want to mess up again."

"I know brother. Your feelings are usually spot on. I will be careful. I am curious who knows about me. If something is off then I'll get rid of them."

Aaron eventually set off to meet with his client. When he arrives, he notices it was one of his clanmates. Aaron's blood begins to boil and balls up his fist.

"Rocks! Why did you send for me?! You better not be wasting my time with some joke or something."

Rocks is known for being the scum of the clan. He was a short common man with a bowl cut hair due. His body was frail and with no muscle tone. The squealing annoying voice Rocks had was weak and no way intimidating. He hasn't been terminated due to his ability to find proper information for the clan. He was known for being a jerk most of the time. No one ever trusts him, especially Aaron.

"Aaron. I know most of the clan don't like me, but I need your help."

"I'm the last person you should have called. I don't like or care for you. I'm leaving."

"Wait! Please. I need someone as strong as you to help me. You see, my wife was taken by a Royal tyrant to be married. I'm sure she doesn't want to be there with such a cruel King. If she is to marry her true King, then he should at least be kind, right. Could you rescue her for me?"

"Why should I trust you Rocks? Plus, you are an assassin as well. Do it yourself."

"Please Aaron. I beg you. I'm not as strong as you are. Look, I even brought a large sack of gold coins for your trouble. Will you help me free her?"

Aaron thinks quietly to himself. "This is stupid. I messed up my last mission by getting that Queen killed. I don't want to be around any other Queens. I hate this but if he's telling the truth then I must take care of that tyrant king and save her."

"Look Rocks. This will be the first and last time I do a job for you, Understood?"

"Yes, yes. I understand."

"I have other matters to attend before I take on this job. I will be taking this money now."

"Of course. Of course."

***

Aaron makes his way back to his home platform. He sneaks into the castle in which his mom was ruling. He wanted to kill the King that stole his mom from him. Knowing that his mom would die Aaron would resort to another option. He would fight him instead. In the distance of the hall Aaron hears moaning coming from the master bedroom. There was a woman stating how much she was loving the sex she was having.

"No! That can't be my mother!"

Aaron didn't care about sneaking anymore. He burst through the doors to find the king mating with his mother.

"Who are you!" The king growled. "I will kill you intruder."

"Mother, how could you forget about me and my father!"

"Aaron!? Is that you? My son, I, I thought you were dead."

"Wait, what? What are you saying? Mother, why would you think that?"

The king and Aaron's mother were dressing when the guards arrived after hearing the commotion. They rush in with their weapons aimed at Aaron.

The King waves his hand at his guards. "Lower your weapons. He is not a threat."

"Aaron, I sent guards to retrieve you long ago. The guards said our home was abandoned. I ordered them to search the farm and villages, but you were nowhere to be found. I heard that Derrick had passed and thought maybe you took your own life from heartbreak."

"Mother, I had no idea. I thought you had abandoned me."

"My son, I would never. I love you forever."

She walks over to Aaron and holds him firmly. "I'm so happy you are alive. Look how handsome you have grown to be."

The tears fell from their face as they embrace one another."

"Aaron. I hope you don't hate me. I love your mother and she told me she had a son. I was prepared to raise you as my own."

Aaron studies the King for a moment seeing he was a kind King and not a tyrant. "I'm not mad at you."

"Thank you. Please allow me to introduce myself. My name is Dillian Dylan the 2nd."

Running between the guards was a small boy that resembled Aaron as a child. The difference with this child is the horns on his head and his glowing purple eyes. Aaron's mother smiles at Aaron and introduces the child.

"Aaron, I would like to introduce you to your brother Dillian Dylan the 3rd."

"I have a little brother. He looks just like me. It's kind of funny."

Aaron's mother giggles. "Yes, he does look like you Aaron. Dillian this is your older brother Aaron."

"Whoa, cool, I have a big brother! It's nice to meet you. Your clothes are so cool. Can I have your hat?"

Aaron chuckles at the small boy. He was full of energy. Aaron gives him a pat on the head and smiles.

"You can't have my hat, but I will give you my scarf if you like."

Aaron places the scarf around his little brother's neck and ties it in a knot.

"Wow! Thank you!"

Dillian Jr. gives his brother a firm hug.

"Mother, I'm so sorry our reunion had to be a bad one. If only I knew."

"Oh boy hush. My son is alive and that's all that matters to me."

"Thank you, mother. But I can't stay long. I have important matters to attend to. I will visit again in a more appropriate way."

Aaron's mother and the king both smiles. The king steps forward and rubs Aaron on the top of his head. Aaron was startled by his actions but didn't fight the familiar feeling. He remembers his father used to do that when he was still alive.

"Aaron you are welcome here anytime."

Aaron's voice softens as he speaks to the King. "Thank you, Sir."

***

Aaron hurries to the next platform to take on Rock's mission. He sneaks into the window which sat a beautiful white-haired Queen.

"She must be from the medical clan." Aaron says in his mind. "She doesn't look like she needs to be rescued. What the heck is going on? Something about this feels off. Cortez told me to listen to my feelings when something doesn't seem right. My goof ball of a brother may seem silly at times but he's never wrong about his feelings."

Aaron creeps behind her. His movement came to a halt. The beautiful Queen turns and spots him. She wasn't afraid.

"I know those clothes very well." She says in a soft gentle voice. "Assassin's clan. If you are here to kill me then you are a lousy assassin." She jokes.

"No, I didn't come to kill you."

The Queen gives a playful giggle. "That's a relief. I couldn't imagine your leaders giving orders to hurt me."

"You know my leaders?"

"Yes, of course I do. They are..."

Before the Queen could answer the door suddenly opens. The Dragon King enters the room and spots Aaron.

"I knew I smelled an unfamiliar scent. Intruder!"

The king extends his claws and lunges toward Aaron. Aaron dodges it but quickly becomes enraged by the sight behind him. The King accidentally stabbed his wife through the chest.

"My...love." The Queen struggles to speak as she touches his face gently and dies in his arms.

"No, No, Noooo!"

The king cries out and falls to his knees. Aaron stabs him in the back and shouts at him.

"You idiot! I wasn't here to kill her! People are going to die because of you. No, because of me... again."

Aaron quickly escapes from the world before it began to crumble killing all who lived there. He set his coordinates back for the assassin's platform. When he arrives, he immediately sprints through the forest.

"She didn't have to die. Not again. I'm not made to do this job."

"Aaron, stop!" Cortez shouts as he quickly catches up to Aaron. "Aaron! Please tell me you weren't the one who killed that Queen."

"No, it was her stupid husband that clawed through her chest. He was aiming for me. I actually talked to her before she died. She was kind. She didn't have to die because of me."

Cortez holds on to Aaron's face and gently speaks to him. "Aaron, I believe you. You need to calm down."

Cortez knew when Aaron was telling the truth and that his feelings were hurt.

"Aaron, who gave you that job?"

"Rocks did."

"Rocks? Aaron, you knew that guy was scum. I just needed to confirm that he did this. Listen, I told you I had a bad feeling, but this is bigger than Rocks."

"What do you mean?"

"I mean, that Queen that died… She was our leaders' little sister and the last of their family."

Aaron skin turn pale, and his breathing comes to a halt. The terror and fear washes over his body like a cold shower.

"No. No! Cortez, I didn't kill her! This is all my fault. They are going to kill me!"

"Aaron, stop blaming yourself! Calm down. I'm going to fix this. Trust me, you will be okay, I promise. For now, keep calm and leave this place now. Take this letter and do this job for me."

"Cortez, I can't do another job. I'll only get more people killed."

"I trust you. Something tells me everything will turn out fine for us. Now go before someone finds you. I will pack your things and leave them at my place. I'm going to get to the bottom of this. Act yourself around the client so he doesn't know your feelings. He may see you as weak or unreliable."

"Thanks bro. I can always count on you to have my back."

"Hey that's what bros are for. Now bring it in."

Aaron hugs Cortez as if he would never see him again and sets off for another mission.

CHAPTER 8

PRISON ESCAPE

Aaron was in the warp cube making his way to a new platform. He rests back in his seat as he relaxes his nerves. While traveling he decides to read the letter Cortez had given him.

"I have to meet with someone named August. Hope he's not another shady guy. Right now, I hope Cortez is able to clear my name. I'm sure he will explain my case to Miquel and Marcel. It's Marcel who I fear the most. I can't think about it. I can't go into my next job worried. People can sense fear in others. I'll just act normal in front of him like Cortez said. I'll take this one last job and that's it. I'm tired of this. I don't feel the same as I did when I first became an assassin. I'm sure Cortez will be fine with my decision of leaving."

Aaron looks out the window to see that he is arriving at his destination. He wonders how this mission would play out for him.

"Well, here I go."

***

Aaron opens his eyes after thinking of his past life. He laughs at himself after remembering all his past decisions which lead him to his life today.

"I was just about to retire after my mission. Now, I have a wife and son I need to get back to. I failed yet another mission and got locked away in this stupid prison. What an outcome. I think I've studied this place long enough though. Now is the time for me to make my move and get the heck out of here."

Aaron peeps over to see the guards were changing shifts. He moves quickly towards the cell door and opens it with the key Luna slipped to him. Aaron silently steps through the halls when the floors start to shift and move like a puzzle. Aaron has been studying the lights that cover the walls and floors of the prison.

"Purple. That seems to be the color the guards always wait for."

Aaron's prediction was spot on as he follows the purple lights as they align on the floors and walls. He pushes forward, following the flow of lights until the sirens went off.

"Looks like they notice I'm missing. This is when things start to get interesting."

As the floors shift once more, Aaron notices a guard waiting on the other side. He gives a mischievous smile.

"Well, looks like today is my lucky day."

Aaron quickly gets behind the guard and snaps his neck. He immediately changes into the uniform the guard was wearing. Aaron notices some keys on the guards.

"I don't know if I'll need these, but I'll take them anyway."

Aaron continues to make his way through the prison when he is stopped by the shifting wall. Two guards were present on the other side. Aaron disguises his voice in a deep low tone.

"I'm in pursuit of the prisoner."

"Of course. You can join our search group. We won't let him escape."

Aaron walks behind the guards until they were distracted by the shift of the floors. He takes the guards' weapons from the side of their waist and stabs one guard in the back. He quickly slices the second guard's throat. On the other side of the shifting walls was a locked door.

"I knew these keys where for something."

Aaron tests each key until he finds the correct one. He opens the door and closes it behind him. Aaron sprints the rest of the way until he sees the exit. There were three guards in front of the door. Aaron knew he had to come up with a plan. He approaches the guards. They signal him to state his business.

"I'm on my way outside to guard the front gates. We can't risk the prisoner's escape."

The guard waves his hand. "Go on ahead."

Aaron sprints out the door and runs as fast as he can when he hears shouting behind him.

"Don't let him get away! He's an imposter!"

Aaron runs even faster towards the side gates. Chasing after him was the guards shadow hounds. The intense blizzard was making Aaron's surroundings impossible to see. Even with the blizzard fighting against him, he was able to make it to the electric fence. He was surprised by his findings. There lying on the ground was a pair of electric proof gloves. He didn't second guess it. He hurries and puts the gloves on and begins to climb the fence. The shadow hounds tried to reach him but couldn't stop in time. They crashed into the fence causing them to be electrocuted.

Aaron makes his way through the freezing forest as fast as he could. He wanted to get as much distance as possible. Infront of him on the ground were sticks in a form of and arrow. The sticks were pointing to the right. Aaron kicks the sticks and runs in that direction.

"Now I'm sure someone is helping me."

He looks to the trees and catches a glimpse of a shadow. Aaron couldn't think about what was happening. As he run through the forest, he spots a tree with a rope lying next to it.

"I can get into the trees with this! That will buy me some time and throw the guards off my trail."

Aaron jumps across the trees when he starts to have a bit of trouble. The trees were slippery with each step. He wonders how whoever was helping him navigated so well. With all the training his mentors gave him, Aaron was able to keep his balance on top of the trees. He knew this mystery person must be skillful to not have slipped on the frozen branches.

After an hour or so of jumping the trees, Aaron stops to rest. He spots a small opening in the rock formation that seems suitable for him to rest in. Aaron jumps down from the trees to catch his breath. The freezing cold was challenging him making every step harder. Lying deep within the opening was a fur blanket made from the fur of a shadow wolf.

"Why is this person helping me? Could it be Cortez? Of course not. With that big mouth of his and way of thinking I would have been caught by now. No, It's someone else. Someone very skilled who can plan ahead. They even knew I would choose this day to escape. Could it be? Never mind, it doesn't matter. They are helping me get back to my family and that's all that's important to me. I can't complain."

Underneath the fur was some water and fruit to eat. Aaron was hungry and exhausted from the journey. He eats and drinks the water as he rests. Over in the corner was a map with a circle around a particular location. The map shows his location and how to make his way over to a warp cube. After much needed rest, Aaron decides it was time to get moving again. He finishes his food and sticks the map in his pocket. He journeys for a few more hours until he comes across a warp cube in the hidden corner of the platform world. Using a bit more of his strength, Aaron sprits towards the cube and sits inside. He set the coordinates for home where Luna was staying.

Aaron takes a deep breath and exhales. He rests his head against the wall and relaxes. The muscles in his legs were throbbing but he didn't care. He had escaped and was making his way through the skies.

"That's it. I'm done with the assassin life. I have responsibilities now, my family."

Aaron was exhausted. He closes his eyes to sleep until he reaches his destination. Hours later he wakes and sees his destination. The Cube lands at the Edge of the backside of the platform. Aaron steps out appreciating being back home again.

"I'll be at my old home in no time. I still remember the shortcuts around here. I can't wait to have that beautiful woman in my arms again."

CHAPTER 9

HER TWO HUSBANDS

A week passed since Aaron arrived at his home world. He travels through the forest until he spots the home he built long ago.

"There it is. I haven't seen my home in a while. I hope Luna has already moved here."

Aaron walks to his home and knocks on the door. He only owned one key which Luna had in her possession.

Luna hears the knock and looks over to Miquel in confusion.

"You should answer the door, Luna. You may be surprised by who's on the other end."

Luna, now curious, went to the door to see who was there. Her heart was filled with a warm loving sensation when she discovers Aaron on the other side. She gasps with excitement when she sees Aaron. "Aaron!"

She leaps into his arms and kisses every part of his face until she finishes with one long passionate kiss. "Aaron, I've missed you so much."

"You have no idea how much I've miss you too, my love."

Aaron grabs Luna by the waist and kisses her will walking into their home. His kiss comes to a halt when he spots Miquel leaning up against the wall. Aaron tries to pretend he didn't know him like he did before.

"Um hello. You're the doctor that helped my wife deliver my child, correct?"

"You can drop the act Aaron. Luna already knows we are familiar with one another."

"Oh, well, okay. Then why are you here? I swear Miquel I didn't murder your sister."

"What! Aaron not again."

Miquel stays as calm as usual. "Luna calm down. I know you didn't murder her. Cortez told me everything. We had evidence that you are innocent. Cortez and I researched the situation together. I know you of all people wouldn't break the assassin's code."

"What's the assassin's code Miquel?"

"One of our codes states that no one is to kill or harm another member's family or anyone they love. If they break this code, then the entire clan will be ordered to hunt and kill whoever broke it."

"You know this because you are a member, right Miquel?"

"He knows because he made the rules. Miquel is one of the leaders of the Shadow Stalkers. The other leader is his brother. They made the clan together long ago."

Luna looks angrily over to Miquel. "More secrets? You know how much I hate that, Miquel. You didn't think I should have known about such important information."

"It wasn't important for you to know at the time. I'm a doctor now so there was no need to bring up the past. I'm sorry I didn't tell you before. I'm just enjoying the life I have now."

"Well, I guess that's okay. I can't stay mad at you anyway."

They both share a smile until Aaron spoke.

"So, I hate to interrupt but, when did the two of you become so close?"

Luna and Miquel look at one another and nod. She walks over to him and locks her fingers with his.

"I am her second husband and father of our two children Aaron."

Aaron stood in silence for a moment. He didn't have the words to say or how to react to the news he had just received.

"Is this the reason why you stopped visiting me Luna?" he asks in a softer tone.

"Yes, and no. I stopped because seeing you locked away forever like that caused my heart pain. I felt so heartbroken being away from you I thought I would have died. I needed to live to see you return. I need to live for Aaron Jr. I thought I was going to die that day they captured you. Then I met Miquel. We grew closer to one another. He was the one who made me happy for all these years. My pain started to fade as we fell in love. The result of him being in my life brought me two more beautiful children. They were born as Royals and Jr. really loves them. They live in the Palace with my friend Eve. Which of course you know as the Queen. You know Miquel discovered that I was a Noble born as well. That's why I'm able to give birth to multiple Royal born babies."

"This is all news to me. I'm happy that you found a way to live and for me. Knowing that you are Noble is surprising as well. So much information I have to process. You know Jr. never stop visiting. He never told me any of this. Maybe he didn't want to anger me or something. He only told me that he would see me free one day. I wonder if he knew I was attempting to escape."

"I did tell him what I was planning the day I slipped you the key Aaron. He never told anyone. I'm just glad you successfully escaped. I never imagined you would escape so easily."

"It was only easy because I had help from you and someone on the platform. He was very skilled and knew every move I was going to take. I wish I could thank that person."

Miquel folds his arms as he speaks. "He probably already knows you are grateful for his help."

"Miquel, it was you, wasn't it? I don't know anyone else who could plan and strategize the way you do."

"Maybe it was me or maybe it wasn't."

Aaron was certain that Miquel was the one helping him escape. He probably doesn't want that information getting out somehow.

"Thank you. I know it was you who assisted me. You don't understand how much this means to me being reunited with Luna."

"You are welcome, Aaron."

Aaron turns to Luna and grabs her waist. He pulls her close and kisses her. He whispers softly in her ear. "I have been waiting eleven years to have you back in my arms again."

Miquel pulls Luna by the arm towards him and holds her close. "I understand your urge Aaron but you're going to have to wait your turn. I was just about to make love to her before you arrived."

Aaron pulls Luna back in his direction and holds her once more. "You've had your turn for years with her." He says gridding his teeth together. "It's my turn. Plus, unlike the clan, I own this woman as I am her first bonded husband."

Miquel pulls her back towards him. "That may be true Aaron. But I am sure Luna knows who really owns her. She tells me all the time."

Both men stare each other down and continue to argue over who was better. They both tugged Luna back and forth until she had enough.

"Hey, why don't you both have me. Both of you are my husband so it shouldn't be a problem. So, let's just make love already."

The men both look at each other and shrug their shoulders. "That's fine with me."

CHAPTER 10

WELCOMING LOVE

Luna begins to rub all over her husbands' bodies. Both men bit their lips as Luna caresses their chests down to their penis. Miquel and Aaron caress her body back and begin gently kissing her neck. Slowly undressing her, the men begin sucking and squeezing her large breast. Their tongues roll around her hard nipples making her moan.

"Ah yes. Both of you don't stop. I love this."

The three of them were making their way towards the bedroom as they were pleasing Luna. She lays back on the bed and enjoy feeling her husbands play with her pussy.

"Mmm, yes. So good."

Aaron enjoys the sight of Luna being pleased. "What a naughty woman you are Luna."

"Yes, I agree. She loves how we're pleasing her."

Luna realizes how nervous her men made her. Her body couldn't help but react to their pleasure and began to tremble. As the men tease her body, she starts to notice them pushing each other's hand away.

She gives both of their hands a slap. "Cut it out both of you, now continue to please me."

Miquel finds her little aggression attractive but quickly puts her back in her place. "Oh, you're giving out orders now? Who gave you permission to tell us what to do?"

Luna speaks nervously. "N- Nobody."

She becomes wetter from the way Miquel speaks to her.

"Hah, she's so wet. You always did like a little dominance, huh Luna?"

"Yes Aaron. I love it when you both take control. It turns me on."

"Then let's continue where we left off, Luna."

"As you wish Miquel."

Luna lays back once more and allows her men to continue. The two men kiss Luna's body down to her pussy. They begin licking slowly, which was driving Luna insane. Luna could barely handle one of them eating her, both were just too much. She could barely handle the pleasure she was receiving. Luna moans loudly as they move their tongues around her pussy.

"Hah! This is too much to handle! So amazing. Please, let me please the both of you as well."

Aaron stands to his feet and stares down at Luna. "Well, I look forward to feeling you, Luna."

Miquel stands as well knowing what Luna was capable of. "I wouldn't mind either."

Luna gets on her knees and begin to stroke both of her men's penis. She begins sucking and stroking back and forth between the two of them. They let out satisfying moans from the way she sucks them. Their eyes roll as she let them go deeper into her mouth. Luna places both their penis in her mouth and begin sucking and rolling around. She loves the way they were strolling their fingers through her long wavy hair.

Aaron bites down on his bottom lip trying to control himself. "Hah, Luna, I can't take this any longer."

"I feel the same. I'm ready to be inside you Luna."

The men lay her on her back and holds her thighs. Aaron lays to the left while Miquel lays to the right of her. They took turns pushing their penis inside her.

"Ah, ah, don't stop. Both of you feel amazing. You're both so hard. I love it."

Miquel eventually pulls Luna to mount on top of him and holds her hips firmly. She starts to ride and bounce slowly on him. He squeezes her ass as she continues to bounce on him.

"Hah yes Luna, you feel amazing right now. Keep going."

Aaron kisses her neck and back as she rides Miquel. Wanting his turn, Aaron starts to slide Luna from Miquel and places her on her hands and knees. He begins thrusting her slowly from the back as he holds onto her hips. Miquel places his penis in her mouth and strokes her hair. Their moans fill the room with the pleasure they were receiving. Her men took turns switching between different positions. Aaron feels himself giving in.

"Man, I can't hold on much longer."

"Neither can I. She feels so good."

Both men continue to pound Luna even faster. Luna's body was shaking uncontrollably as they stroked her. Her moans became louder and louder. Miquel and Aaron pull out of her and releases their cream over her breast. Luna tries to catch her breath.

"That was amazing. More than I could handle. Both so amazing."

"Yes, it was." they both say.

Luna once again becomes nervous around her men. "I think I'm going to go take a shower."

She runs quickly to the shower not looking back.

"Wait she wasn't this nervous just a minute ago."

"Well Aaron, looks like with both of us being here together made her more nervous than she thought. I'll go join her in the shower to calm her nerves."

Aaron squints his eyes at Miquel. He speaks with his teeth tight together. "No, I will join her."

Both men stare at each other intensively until Miquel runs quickly to join Luna. Aaron chases after him.

"Miquel, stop! You already had your time with her!"

CHAPTER 11

TAKEN

Luna wakes up the next morning. She looks over to see Aaron sleeping on her right while Miquel was sleeping on her left. She smiles in appreciation for having such loving husbands. Trying not to wake them, Luna slides down the middle of the bed.

"I think they both deserve a morning meal after what they did last night."

Luna walks to the kitchen to prepare their morning meal. As she cooks, she notices Miquel and Aaron entering the room.

"Wow, that smells amazing! This will be the first time I get to taste your cooking, Luna. This definitely will be better than that prison food."

"Oh yeah, you're right Aaron, it would be! Back then you would come and go. You never had time to eat my food. Well, this should be refreshing for you, my love. I will serve you and Miquel a plate right away."

She cheerfully serves them their meal and gives them a kiss on the cheek. "Enjoy my loves."

"Mm, thank you Luna. This is delicious. I should have been around more often."

"You must have put a lot of love and effort into this. I can't imagine what brought this on." Miquel says, giving Luna a wink.

"I think you both know the answer to that."

The men stare at Luna's ass as she walks away. The way her hips moved put a smile on both their faces. The three of them sat eating their meal not knowing that August had arrived at the front door.

"Ah, finally I made it to Luna's house. What a strange and secluded area she has chosen. Doesn't matter where she lives; I have her all to myself."

August was suddenly grabbed from behind before he could knock on the door. There were three men who had their faces covered by their cloaks as they wrestle August to the ground. One of the hooded men knocks August over the head making him unconscious. The men put a sack over his head and carries him off into the darkness of the Twisted Forest. The third man leaves a note at the front of the door. He gives a hard knock at the front door before fleeing.

Miquel and Aaron quickly rise from their seats and pull out their weapons.

"Whoa, what's going on?"

"Luna, no one should know of this location. I chose this location knowing it would be hard to find."

Miquel looks over to the door with a serious expression. "Aaron is right, somethings off about this. That knock was not normal even if someone did find this location. Luna, stay back until we know what's going on."

"Okay, sure."

Aaron and Miquel nodded at each other and crept up to the door. Aaron slowly opens it and peaks out the opening. "No one's here."

"Aaron, stay on guard. Someone might still be around. They wouldn't knock the way they did and just flee."

"I don't get it either Miquel, but they did leave a note."

"Aaron if you want to see your brother alive then come to the assassin's location."

Signed Marcel

"What! This note was left by Marcel's men! It says he has my brother. Miquel, what is the meaning of this? I thought we cleared up everything about your sister. Could he still be upset with me?"

"Hmm, this is rather strange. My brother wouldn't do this without reason. I will have to look into the matter. Cortez and I made sure we handled this situation."

Luna walks to the door from behind them wanting to see what was happening. She sees a bag in front of the door. "Wait. Why is that bag here?"

Miquel grabs Luna's arm trying to pull her away from the door, "Luna, stay back! This could be a trap."

"No, that's August bag."

"August!" they both say.

"Yes, I made that bag for him when we were young. The men didn't take your brother, they took August."

"They must have mistaken him for my little brother. Well, if it's that guy they took then let them have him."

"Aaron, how could you say that? He's my friend and is innocent in this situation. We have to rescue him."

"We are talking about the assassin's clan, my love. They are skilled well-trained men. They're not going to hand August over easily, especially if this is an order from my brother."

"There's no other explanation for this Miquel. Marcel must still be angry with me. I took that job. I was the reason this happened in the first place. I'm to blame."

"Enough putting blame on yourself Aaron!" he says grudgingly. "I hate it when you get all emotional like that. Now, let's think for a moment. There must be something we're missing about this situation. Either way, we are going to need some help with this matter. We need someone just as skilled as we are Aaron, if you catch my meaning."

"Yeah, I get what you mean. Let's go see Cortez."

CHAPTER 12

BROTHERS REUNION

Luna, Aaron, and Miquel were quickly making their way through the Twisted Forest. Luna was being carried on the back of Miquel as he jumped through the trees.

"Miquel, are you sure you are not tired of carrying me?"

"You're fine Luna. I've trained to carry much heavier things for an even longer period of time. So just relax my love. You're not a burden."

The three of them traveled the trees for a few more miles until they spotted Cortez's land.

"We made it! It's been a while since I've been to my bro's farm."

They jump down from the trees. Cortez's massive farmland was a sight of unimaginative beauty. The land was filled with grains, fruits, and veggies as far as the eyes could see. Every plant was lined neatly across the fields. There was a barn in the distance which held all the rare shadow creatures. Cortez has tamed and raised many shadow beings over the years. Luna studies the land. Her eyes wander with excitement and amazement.

"Wow, this land is so beautiful! Look at all the different shadow creatures around here!"

"Yeah, this is just what I would imagine from Cortez. He's very clean and is a vegetarian that cares for nature and his creatures. I never seen anyone who loves the lands and animals as much as my bro does."

"He sounds like a really nice guy Aaron."

Miquel chuckles. "He is kind, Luna. Once you meet him you will see that he is different than everyone else. We can't forget his rare appearance as well."

Luna continues to look out into the farm when she spots a man in the distance tending to the garden. He had on his black overalls and a tight white shirt underneath that showed off his abs and muscles. Luna tries not to make it obvious that she was checking out his body.

"Is that him over there?"

"Yeah, that's him Luna. Hey Cortez, over here!"

"Aaron!?"

Cortez runs across the field to Aaron and hugs him firmly. "Boss! You're here too? Come on bring it in."

"No Cortez. What have I told you about hugging."

Before Miquel could run, he ends up in the arms of Cortez. He squeezes him tightly with a big smile across his face. Miquel rolls his eyes at his actions.

"Oh, goodness, you're just as friendly as ever."

"Well, I missed you boss. Ever since you became a doctor, I never get a chance to see you often. You know you're like a father who abandoned his child."

"How dare you say such a thing!"

Miquel tries not to laugh at Cortez's actions and words. He always felt a sense of happiness every time he was in his presence.

Cortez spots Luna and smiles at her. "Oh, and who is this lovely woman?"

"This woman is my wife and Aaron's as well."

"Wait, she's married to both of you? You naughty men. I bet you have lots of fun if you know what I mean."

Cortez gives them a wink and grins. Aaron and Miquel ignore his silly jokes and roll their eyes.

Cortez turns back to look at Luna. He was always nervous when meeting new people especially women. Even while shy, Cortez would always be friendly to others first.

"Hello there beautiful. Name's Cortez."

Luna stares at him for a moment. She was lost for words at that moment. Cortez couldn't help but wonder in his mind how this interaction would turn out.

"Well, here we go again. I might as well get ready to be called a freak or weird again."

"Your hair is red! I've never seen anyone who looks like you before. It's so long and beautiful. Can I touch it?"

"Uh, yeah." he says shyly. "You can touch my hair if you like."

Cortez was not expecting such a kind reaction from Luna. No woman has ever complimented him or even cared to look his direction. He couldn't comprehend the emotions he was feeling. His body feels warm from her touch as she strolls her fingers through his hair. Luna could tell by his body language that he was nervous from her presence. She places her hand gently on his cheek as she stares into his gentle eyes.

"You don't have to be afraid. You are so beautiful."

Cortez almost fell apart from her consideration and gentle touch. He places his hand over hers and stares back into her eyes.

"Thank you, Luna." he says in a soft shy tone.

Luna's eyes studied Cortez for a moment, she was feeling oddly attracted to him. She thinks to herself for a moment.

"My goodness. How do I keep running into these sexy men. I better pull away from him before Miquel and Aaron notice me."

"Cortez. I will be leaving Luna with you and Aaron's care. I only accompanied Aaron to make sure Luna made it here safely. I have to go investigate something. Aaron and Luna will explain and give you the details on what is happening."

Luna takes on a concerning look. "Wait you're leaving Miquel?"

"Yes, my love. Don't worry about me. You are in good hands with the two of them together. Their teamwork and skills are just as good as mine and my brother's. We trained them well, so I trust they will protect you while I'm away."

"Okay but come back soon okay."

"I will, my love."

Miquel gives her a long loving kiss before he disappears into the darkness of the forest.

"Well, this is exciting! You two can make yourselves at home. I'm just amazed that you were able to break out of prison so soon bro. To be honest, I had a feeling that you would make it out okay."

"I had to thank Luna and Miquel for their assistance. Luna slipped me a key years ago and Miquel navigated me off of the platform. I probably wouldn't have made it out alive if it wasn't for the two of them."

"Wow, you really do have an amazing wife. That takes guts to help Miquel is something so dangerous and risky."

"Yeah, she is amazing. Now, let's get inside. I need to rest from our long journey."

"Sure, let's go. I have plenty of rooms in my mansion."

Aaron walks in front of Luna and Cortez ready to get some rest. Luna, walking behind Aaron, couldn't help but look back to admire

Cortez again. Cortez sees her eyeballing his abs and body. She gives him a wink and continues to walk. Cortez quickly notices Luna's ass swinging left to right in a very pleasing way.

"Oh my. She likes to tease I see. She is such a naughty woman."

CHAPTER 13

HOME WELCOMING

"So, I already have rooms prepared for guests." Cortez says. "The two of you can have this room. It's large enough and has its own bathroom. Aaron, you can rest up first then tell me what's going on afterwards."

"Thanks bro. I really can use the rest. My body can't stand much longer. What about you Luna? Are you coming to join me?"

"Not yet. I would like to explore this massive home. I've never seen a place like this before. If that's okay with you Cortez?"

"I'm okay with it. You can explore as much as you like."

"Thank you. You are so kind. I can't wait to see all the beauty of your home."

"Enjoy exploring his home, Luna. I will be here if you need me. See you in a bit Cortez."

"Sure thing bro.

Aaron takes his leave and flops on the bed to rest. His body ached from the long journey they had.

"I think I'll go take a shower. I've been working in the garden all day. See ya Luna."

"Sure, see ya handsome." she says giving him a little wink.

Cortez tries his best not to grab Luna and kiss her from all the flirting she was doing. Instead, he gives her a shy smile and walks away.

Luna was left alone to enjoy the mansion. "Well, which room should I check out first? Looking at the halls and the floral of this house is extremely eye-catching. The purple and blue glowing flowers are one of my favorites of this platform. His place feels like it's one with nature. It's nothing like any other home I've seen before. He's so clean and tidy."

Luna makes her way through every room in the house until she reaches Cortez's master bedroom.

"I'm sure he wouldn't mind if I peek in his room for a moment. I bet it's nice inside."

She slowly and quietly opens the door and steps inside. She talks softly so Cortez wouldn't hear her.

"Oh wow, this room is huge! Look at all the plants and lighting. That bed looks like it was made for the King and Queen."

As Luna creeps through the room, she notices the shower still running. Not able to help her curiosity, she begins slowly opening the door to have a look inside. Luna's body becomes hot as she clearly sees Cortez naked body. She bites down on her lip as she watches the water roll off his well-toned wet body. His hair was long and flowed down to his tight ass and tone back. Cortez turns to the side to grab his soap exposing his large penis to Luna. She gasps quietly.

"Oh, my goodness."

Trying to catch her breath, Luna fails to notice that Cortez could see her through his hidden mirror installed in his shower. Due to being an assassin he must always watch his back from others. He watches as Luna starts to feel and touch her body and breast as she watches him shower. Cortez becomes aroused by the sight of her actions. His penis hardens as he strokes himself to her. Luna loves what she was seeing and how slow and firm Cortez strokes himself. She lifts her dress and pulls down her panties slightly. She began rubbing her already wet pussy. Both play with themselves as they watch each other. They relieve themselves at the same time.

"I must hurry and leave before he sees what I've done."

Luna rushes out of the room to go clean herself. Cortez looks back at the door and smiles.

"Man, I really want that woman."

***

After Luna took a bath, she noticed she was overwhelmingly hungry after the long journey. She looks around the kitchen to grab a bite to eat. She opens the fridge to find nothing but fresh healthy foods from Cortez's Garden.

"This man surprises me every time. All he eats is natural fresh foods from his fields. Maybe that's how he keeps that hot body looking so good."

Luna reaches into one of the cabinets to grab a plate when Cortez sneaks up behind her. He grabs her hips and pulls her towards his body. He feels and squeezes all over her while holding her close. Luna's eyes roll as he kisses her neck all the way to her ear. He whispers in her ear.

"I saw what you did, Luna."

"Hah, Cortez. What, what do you mean?"

"I caught you feeling on that sexy body of yours when I was taking a shower. You must of really like what you saw, didn't you?"

Luna's eyes continue to roll as Cortez continues to feel on her body while rubbing his hard penis up against her ass.

"Hah, yes Cortez. I like what I saw."

"Oh, well, I like what I saw as well."

Cortez continues to feel on her body while kissing on her neck and shoulder.

"Mmm… Cortez your lips are so soft. I want more. I can't fight this connection I'm feeling."

"I am having the same feeling. I need you."

He feels on her breast and sucks her neck making her moan. He turns her around and sits her on the countertop. Standing between her legs, he slips his tongue into her mouth as he gently kisses her. Luna moans as she kisses him and plays in his hair. Their kiss comes to a stop when they hear the door open in the distance.

"Aaron is done resting."

"Yeah, I guess he is. I will have to finish with you at another time Luna."

"I will be looking forward to that, Cortez."

Cortez sits Luna back onto the floor and walks over to grab some food. Aaron walks through the door moments later.

"Hey there bro. You look well rested."

"Yeah, it was needed. Did you finish touring the house, Luna?"

"Yes, every room was magnificent. This is a very lovely home Cortez has."

"That's good. Glad you've enjoyed yourself. Now that I'm awake it's time for us to discuss some important business."

CHAPTER 14

PLAN FOR AN IMPOSSIBLE RESCUE

"Cortez, the reason we are here is to ask for your help. The assassins were ordered by Marcel to threaten me into turning myself him."

"Are you serious? You should have been in the clear. Miquel and I already investigated the truth of the situation."

"Well, that doesn't mean anything to Marcel apparently. He even went through the trouble of abducting Luna's friend August. They were under the impression that he was my little brother."

"August. August. Why does that name sound familiar? Wait, that was the guy who gave me the job that I handed off to you."

Aaron speaks sarcastically as he rolls his eyes. "Yeah, thanks for that. You really changed my life for better and worst."

"You're welcome! Snagging a beautiful wife and starting a family seems worth it, don't you think?"

"Yeah, it was worth it."

"You guys are so sweet. So, what do you say Cortez, will you help us rescue August?"

"Hmm, going up against the assassin's clan is no easy task. Marcel is the one I'm most worried about. Aaron and I know the skill and pure power he wields. He's dangerous and not as understanding as Miquel. Even though, he's just as dangerous."

"I know what you mean Cortez. For all we know August might already be dead and they are just using him as bait."

The men didn't realize their words had sadden Luna. They see her eyes start to water from the thought that August may be dead. Both Cortez and Aaron move closer to comfort her.

"Luna don't cry. There is still like a 1% chance that he's still alive."

Aaron smacks Cortez in the back of the head and frowns at him.

"Cortez, could you be and idiot at another time."

"Hey, if Luna met Marcel, she would understand that I gave her I lot of hope just now."

"Cortez, please help me get my friend back."

Luna pleads with tears flowing down her cheek. Cortez couldn't bear to see her sad. He wipes the tears from her face and looks into her watery eyes. He speaks softly to her.

"Yes, Luna. I will do anything for you."

Luna stands and wraps her arms around Cortez. "Thank you. You are truly amazing."

"You're welcome, Luna."

"Thank you, Cortez, for helping her. Now that we have you on board with this, I need us to come up with a plan."

"Well first, I need to inform you that the hideout has been relocated. I left the clan after I finished helping them move. So, I know the layout of the building and surrounding area pretty well. Every now and then I may go back to check things out. Staying out of the loop permanently would be dumb."

"Where do you suppose they are keeping August?"

"They're probably holding him in the cellar below the base. They have two floors, one for the clan members and the other is a personal floor for Marcel. His floor is on the top of course."

"How will we infiltrate this cellar?"

"We have two options, the first being that I walk through the door find the key and steal it. Or we kill whoever stands in our way at the entrance and make things go a little quicker. That is before Marcel shows up and kick our ass."

"Hm, let's go with the second option."

"I knew you would choose that one bro."

CHAPTER 15

PREPARATIONS

"Luna, you should stay here and wait for me and Cortez's return."

"No, I'm going with you guys."

"Luna don't be crazy! This isn't some walk in the woods! This is the assassin's clan we're talking about. You can get killed."

Luna crosses her arms. "Oh, and I thought you two were the best assassins other than your leaders. I should be perfectly safe in you guys' care. That's what Miquel said, right? I am going even if I have to hide in the forest. I want to see all three of you make it through this safely."

"Fine, stubborn woman, but you will need to stay hidden no matter what. This mission is dangerous even for Cortez and I."

"I know of a spot where she will be safe. They don't patrol certain areas of the forest so this spot will be perfect."

"Are you sure she'll be safe Cortez?"

"I guarantee she will be fine. I wouldn't jeopardize her life Aaron."

"Alright then, we should get moving. The sooner we leave the better our chances of finding August alive."

Aaron, Luna, and Cortez traveled through the forest until they were close enough to the assassins' hideout. The night sky became even darker which camouflaged them perfectly into the shadowed trees.

"Cortez, take Luna to the spot you talked about. Keep her safe no matter what."

"Sure thing bro. Come Luna, follow me."

Cortez and Luna run to the hidden location far from the assassins' hideout. Luna spots the largest tree she has ever seen. The area of the forest was covered with twisted vines and mist. The plant life submerges the opening of the tree like a hidden doorway. It would be hard for anyone unfamiliar with the area to spot them.

"There it is Luna; I want you to hide in this tree for me."

"This tree is massive Cortez. How could they not notice a place like this?"

"This tree seems large, but it's well hidden behind the mist and vines. They don't like navigating through such a dense thorny area. You can easily get lost if you don't know your way around. I've spent years studying these landscapes they've failed to observe."

Cortez and Luna finally reach the tree which had the opening that Luna could hide in. Before she walks through, Cortez pulls her back to him and gives her a long-lasting kiss. She wraps her arms around him as she kisses him back. Luna catches her breath after such a passionate kiss.

"Hah Cortez, you better be safe and return back to me."

"I will make sure I do beautiful. I want to be bonded to you. My feelings never lie. It's telling me how special you are to me. Now hide, I will see you soon once we find your friend."

Cortez quickly makes his way back to where Aaron was hiding."

"Is she safe?"

"Yep, I made sure to scout the area just to make sure."

"Good, so what's our strategy?"

"First, we have to make it to the back entrance where the cellar is located. We need to sneak behind the guards and take them out. After we take them out there will be at least four to six men inside guarding August cell. Soon as they are taken care of, we grab the keys off their bodies and free this August guy."

"I'm sure it's not going to be as easy as you make it sound Cortez."

"Hey, it never is bro. Now let's make our move while the night is at its darkest."

The men make their way toward the side of the building where they spot two guards at the front entrance of the cellar. Aaron and Cortez were around long enough to know how the clan operates. They both look to the trees and spot two more assassins guarding the entrance. Aaron hand signals for them to take out the assassins up in the trees first. Aaron and Cortez's stealth was top notch. The guards didn't hear them sneak into the trees. Before they knew it their necks were broken simultaneously.

Aaron and Cortez silently laid the men's body on the tree and took their bows and arrows. They ready their bows and take aim at the guards at the front entrance. Aaron nods for them to shoot down the guards. The arrows went straight through their chest killing them instantly. Aaron and Cortez jump down from the trees. Cortez searches the bodies for the entrance key.

"Found it. You ready bro?"

"Yep. Let's do this."

CHAPTER 16

A RESCUE GONE WRONG

Aaron and Cortez carefully opened the door and creeped inside. The basement of the building was dark with barely any light coming from the candles mounted on the walls. Cortez counts the assassins guarding the halls. He holds up four fingers to Aaron.

Down the hall August was being mistreated. The assassins were punching and pouring freezing water over him.

"This guy is pathetic." one of the assassins says. "Are we sure this guy is related to Aaron?"

"Please. I'm not the person you're looking for. I don't even have a brother."

"Shut up scum!" The second assassin says as he punches August in the face.

Aaron and Cortez were making their way down the dark halls to the first two assassins. They choke the guys from behind and silently sits their bodies down. Aaron and Cortez hid behind the side wall from where August was being held. When the assassins exited the cell, they were quickly stabbed through the heart.

August was still in a panic especially after seeing the assassins being killed. "Who's there?! Who are you?!"

Cortez rushes to cover August mouth. "Oh, my goodness. Shut up. Are you trying to get us killed? We were sent by Luna to rescue you. "

"Wait, you over there. You're the assassin!"

Cortez slaps August in the face and holds him up by the collar.

"Look here you asshole. If I get caught trying to rescue an idiot like you then I will spare no time killing you."

"Sorry, please don't hurt me. I've already been through enough. I just don't understand how he's here. He supposed to be locked away for life."

"Well, if you feel that way then I could just leave your ass here to die."

"No, I'm sorry. Please get me out of here."

Cortez and Aaron start to communicate without words about August. Cortez looks at Aaron in a confused way and points to August. Aaron rolls his eyes nodding yes, this is Luna's idiot friend. Cortez unties August and shoves him out of the cell.

"Hurry Aaron, we need to get out of here now!"

They almost made it out of the dungeon when they were spotted by another assassin. Aaron frowns and pulls out a dagger.

"Damn it! Kill him now!"

The assassin had already blown the horn before Aaron threw the dagger at his heart.

"We have to run!" Both Aaron and Cortez shout.

They knew if and clanmate blows the horn it means business. All the assassins will rally at the sound of it. The three men run as fast as they can to the exit. Cortez and Aaron could already see the shadow figures jumping through the trees. Arrows were being shot in their direction from the darkness of the forest. The men run out into the forest thinking of a plan.

"Cortez, it's too many of them. We have to split up. Go get Luna and get her to safety."

"You got it bro. Meet me at my yacht down at the river. Go to the spot we talked about."

"Wait! We're splitting up?! I can't fight these guys, I'm not like the two of you!"

Aaron was irritated by August words. "That's why we're running stupid. Now split!"

The men split into different direction to shorten the numbers between them. Aaron runs even faster to a spot where he can defend himself. Four assassins jump down from the trees surrounding Aaron. Aaron was familiar with the fighting formation they were using. He easily dodges and weaves through their attacks, cutting them down one after another. There was a reason he was one of the best. He has always had an advantage over the other clan members. His only struggle was with Miguel and Marcel. Aaron knew he didn't want to come face to face with his former leader Marcel. He would die for sure he thought in his mind. Aaron knew he had to continue escaping through the forest once he finished fighting the assassins.

Over on the other end of the Twisted Forest August continues to run for his life. He was starting to become exhausted not having the stamina Aaron and Cortez have. August, not knowing if he was still being followed looks back to check his surroundings. Out of nowhere he found himself falling through a giant hole in the ground. He continues to fall until he splashes in the water below. The assassins who were following him had lost his tracks.

"Do you see him?" One of the assassins asks.

"No. But there's no way he could have gone far. Split up and find him."

August emerges from the waters below and swims to the shore of the cave he was in. He lays back and takes the time to catch his breath. August looks up at the giant hole above. He knew there was no way of climbing back to the top.

"I wonder if those two escaped. Damn it. Why is that assassin out of prison? I think I remember his name being Aaron or something. What the heck is going on? I get that Luna sent them but how? Is she ok? What if the assassins find her. This is too much to process, I've never been in any situation like this before. I need to rest then find my way out of here."

***

While August rested, Aaron and Cortez were still on the run. Cortez was rushing to get to Luna. He finally makes it to the tree where he left her. He reaches for her hand and pulls her to run with him.

"Hey beautiful. We got to go, now."

Cortez was running so fast that Luna could barely keep up.

"Cortez, I can't run as fast as you."

Cortez didn't hesitate to swoop Luna onto his back and continue to run.

"Cortez, what happened? Where is Aaron and August?"

"I'll explain later, love. Right now, we have to run."

Cortez stops in his tracks before slipping off a massive waterfall. He places Luna on the ground so they can look at what they were dealing with. The waterfall was steep, about 70 feet at least. Cortez scratches his head trying to think of a plan.

"Oh man, this could be a problem."

He looks behind him to see four of the assassins behind them.

"Give up Cortez you can't run from us." The man says.

Cortez recognizes the man's voice. "Wait a minute. Tazz, is that you? Jack, Roger, you're here too? And you over there, well, I don't know you, so whatever."

"Yes, it's us Cortez." Tazz says. "You know you're going to have to turn yourself in to Marcel."

"Really? Out of all the assassins, you guys are going to turn me in? Tazz, when your mom broke her leg who went out to find the healing herbs for her?"

"What? Well, you did. Cortez don't do this."

"No, we're doing this Tazz. Jake, when your family was starving who brought them food from his garden?"

"You did." he says in a monotone voice.

"Oh, and I can't forget you, Roger. When you were too scared to talk to that woman you love, who gave you the courage?"

"Okay, okay. It was you." he says folding his arms."

The other two men folded their arms and sighs.

"What are you guys doing?" The fourth assassin says. "Let's get this guy!"

The assassin rushes Cortez trying to stab him. Cortez trips and stabs the man through the chest.

"O, kay? Who was this guy again? Marcel running low on good help or something?"

"He was a rookie. Now he's dead thanks to you." Tazz replies.

The three assassins look at one another. They knew Cortez to be kind but vicious when he's serious. They didn't want to die by his hands.

"You know what. I think it's time to retire."

The other two men agree with Tazz and drop their weapons.

"See ya around Cortez. We're going back to our families."

"Bye Tazz, bye guys! Have a safe journey home."

Luna stands beside Cortez with her mouth wide. She couldn't believe that Cortez had just talked his way out of that situation.

"Careful Luna, you keep holding your mouth open like that then I'm going to have to put something in it."

Luna punches Cortez in the arm as she blushes. "You are so naughty. Now tell me what happened at the hideout."

Before Cortez can explain, they both see a group of assassins heading their way.

"Luna, you're going to hate me for this, but we are going to have to jump."

"What!? Are you crazy? There could be deadly rocks at the bottom of this waterfall."

"We don't have a choice. I can't fight with you around. You could get killed."

"This is crazy."

The men were closing in on their location as Luna stares down the waterfall. Cortez quickly grabs Luna and jumps off the cliff. Luna screams for dear life.

"Cortez, I'm going to kill you!"

CHAPTER 17

THE 3RD HUSBAND

Cortez and Luna splashed at the bottom of the waterfall. Cortez notices Luna wasn't moving and immediately swims to the shore. He lays her motionless body on her back and pulls her into the forest to be hidden from the other assassins.

"Luna?" he whispers. "No, Luna please wake up?"

Cortez pleads as his eyes begin to water. "You can't die after I finally found someone to love."

Cortez immediately starts breathing slightly into Luna's mouth trying to get the water out of her lungs. He stays calm until she can breathe again. Luna finally coughs the water from her body. Cortez smiles while turning her to her side so she can recover. The situation was frightening to him. He was about to lose someone he deeply cared for.

"Cor…tez." she says softly.

She looks up to Cortez seeing the tears flow down his face. A smile comes across her face as she looks at him. She gently wipes his face not wanting to see him sad.

"Cortez. I'm okay now. Thanks to you we are alive and safe from those men."

"That's not the point Luna. I…I thought I was going to lose you. I love you. Seeing you lifeless like that broke my heart. I will never want to see you in danger like that again."

"Cortez, your words are warming to my heart. I love you too ya know. I still want to kill you for making me jump but here we are. You've protected me so far and you didn't have to risk your life to save my friend, but you did. You are amazing."

Cortez let out a slight laugh and holds her close. Her words meant so much to him. Her sense of humor was refreshing to him. Looking up, Cortez can see the assassins had changed direction. They assumed no one would ever be crazy enough to jump off a waterfall that size.

"Luna, I think we are in the clear, but we should still wait for a bit until you recover."

"That's fine but we can't stay long. The night is only getting darker, and the wind is starting to pick up. We are soaked and need to get dry soon."

"You're right. Here, let me carry you. I don't want you in anymore trouble."

Cortez picks up Luna from the ground and holds her legs and waist. They follow the riverbank as well as staying hidden in the forest's shadows. Cortez sees his yacht floating in the distance as they walk.

"There's the yacht Luna. We need to get these clothes off fast. I have a heater that can dry your clothes for you. You will have to be naked for a while though."

"I'm okay with being naked."

Cortez tries to hold back his smile as he was already distracted by Luna's body. He already can see right through her wet shirt which expose her breast and hard nipple. Luna on the other hand stares at his body as well seeing his abs through his shirt.

Cortez looks around once again. He had to make sure no one was hidden in the forest before he places Luna down. They step inside the warm cozy yacht and exhale.

"What a nice yacht you have here. Do you have a shower on it?"

"Matter a fact I have two. You can use the one down the hall to the left while I use the one on the right."

The two of them enjoy getting into the warm waters, washing off the river water from the waterfall. They meet up in the master bedroom with only towels covering their bodies. They stand silently admiring each other's body for a moment.

"Forget this. I can't take it anymore Luna."

Cortez makes his way over to Luna and grabs her face and kisses her. Luna moans as he gives her a sloppy but satisfying kiss. His mouth devours her lips as their tongues intertwine with one another. Luna's eyes roll. She has never had a kiss quite like this before. Her body temperature rises as he makes out with her.

Cortez removes the towels from him and Luna and throws them to the floor. Luna holds him tight as he sucks and kiss her neck down to her breast. Luna's body quivers every time she feels his soft lips against her body. He lays her on the bed and starts to kiss and suck her feet.

"Hah, Cortez. I love that."

"Well then, allow me to give you more."

Cortez mounts Luna on his face as he lay flat on the bed. He moves her body so she may ride his face while he kisses and licks her.

"Oh, my goodness." she whispers. "Your head is amazing. I can feel your entire mouth devouring my pussy."

Her body trembles as she rides his face slowly. Looking down, she sees Cortez hard penis.

"Hah, so fat and long. I want to taste you as well."

Luna leans forward and begin licking and sucking his penis. Cortez's body reacts to the sudden pleasure he was receiving from her. He moans when she sucks him faster.

"Hah, Luna, slow down. I'm not trying to cum yet."

Luna ignores him and continues. Hearing him moan satisfies her. Cortez couldn't handle much more of it. He quickly flips her to her back and lays between her thighs. Not wasting any time, he slides his penis inside her. Cortez almost lost his mind when he felt how warm and wet, she was. Luna wraps her legs around him as he takes his time stroking her. Every moan Luna makes was driving him crazy.

"Luna, you feel amazing. I'd never imagine feeling pleasure like this before."

"I feel the same. Your love making is driving me insane. Go deeper, please."

"As you wish."

The deeper Cortez went the louder Luna's moan became.

"Ah Yes! Keep going Cortez! Hah, I love you so much!"

"Luna, I love you too."

Cortez flips her to her stomach and pushes inside her. He takes pleasure grinding on her fat ass as he kisses her back.

"More!" she says as her voice quivers. "I love what you're doing to me Cortez. I want to return the favor."

"Oh really. Then how about you get on top of me."

"I would love to ride you, Cortez."

She slowly sits and slides him inside her. Both their eyes roll as she rides him slowly. He couldn't help gripping her ass as she grinds on him.

"Ah, Cortez! I can't handle your large penis."

"Yes, you can. Please keep going."

Luna's legs start to shake uncontrollably at this point. Her breathing flutters as she tries to handle Cortez's penis.

"Yes, Luna! Keep going. I'm about to release so hard inside you."

"I can't. You are too much for me."

"You better not stop Luna."

Cortez pulls her down to him, they kiss as he pushes deeper inside of her. He bounces her faster and pushes even deeper causing Luna to scream. She screams his name repeatedly as he accelerates his speed. He holds her tight as he relieves himself inside of her. Their symbol of bonding love emerges on both of their backs.

"Cortez, I am yours now."

"Yes, you are, and I belong to you."

"Have to be honest Cortez. I wanted to bond with you the moment I met you. I had this feeling that you belong to me."

"I had the same feeling, Luna. Bonds are strong. The connection of love the people have go way back before we were even born. I find nothing wrong with it. I'm just glad after all these years I've finally found you."

"Oh no, what will Aaron think."

"Oh, Aaron's not going to think anything. He's going to kill me Luna."

CHAPTER 18

A FIGHT AMONG BROTHERS

Back deep in the Twisted Forest, Aaron was finishing off the last assassin that was chasing him.

"Finally. It felt like every assassin was focused on me for some reason. Now, I need to keep moving towards where Luna and Cortez are. I hope they're safe. Hmm, why am I worrying. Luna is in great hands. If anyone could protect her it would be him. I have to pick up the speed before anyone else shows up. Cortez should already have the yacht running so we can get away. It's going to be awhile before I catch up to them. Thanks to those assholes who wouldn't stop attacking me I'm running late. Don't worry Luna, I'll be there soon."

The following morning Aaron was still making his way to the yacht. Cortez wakes that morning snuggled up with Luna.

"Man, I can't believe this woman is mines too. She's so beautiful. I wouldn't mind making love to her again before Aaron arrives."

Luna wakes as she feels Cortez stroking her hair. She smiles at him and kisses his lips.

"Hey there beautiful." he says softly. "How did you sleep?"

"I slept well, thanks to you."

Cortez kisses her once more.

"Hah, Cortez, I just love how gentle you kiss me. I can't get enough."

"I could say the same about your kiss. How about we take a shower and I prepare you something to eat."

"I would love that, but you still haven't told me what happened back at the assassins' hideout. Aaron still isn't here yet. I know he's alright because I would have felt something was wrong."

"You're right. I need to tell you what happened. We ended up getting spotted by one of the clan members. He blew a horn that alerts the other members for reinforcements. We successfully freed August but had to split up soon after. We were surrounded by too many assassins. We both know Aaron is fine but to be honest, August may be dead."

"Cortez, stop. Let's not lose hope so quickly. I know August. He won't die that easily."

"I hope you are right. These are skilled men we are talking about. We will just have to wait and see. Now, let's start our day, okay. Aaron should be returning soon."

"Okay."

Luna and Cortez had finished their showers and went to prepare their meal. Luna helps in the kitchen while watching Cortez cook. She prepares the table and sits to enjoy her food.

"This is pretty good Cortez. I'm still trying to get familiar with this kind of cooking."

"I can teach you more once this is all over."

"That would be so kind of you."

"So, um Luna. You want to go another round?"

"Absolutely."

They both walk to the bedroom and start to make out. Luna sucks Cortez's neck while he feels on her ass. They suddenly stop when they hear footsteps on top of the yacht.

"Luna, you need to..."

Cortez was interrupted when the power was shut down and the lights went dark. He hears Luna scream and quickly cut on his emergency lights. He found three assassins in his room with the third taking Luna. He wrestles with the other two men punching them to the ground. He grabs his weapon and stabs the first assassin. He pulls the other up, holding his collar.

"Where did that other guy take my wife!"

"I will never tell." The man says struggling to stand. "Marcel will kill me otherwise."

"How about I do it instead."

Cortez jabs the man in the side with his dagger.

"Ahhh. Please, please don't kill me. I'll talk. They are taking her back to Marcel. She's going to be his hostage."

"Thank you for that. Since you just betrayed Marcel, I'm going to have to kill you now."

Cortez stabs the man in the chest and drops him to the ground.

Aaron, seconds later, arrives at the yacht. He notices the engine wasn't running. He quickly rushes inside.

"Cortez! Luna! Where are you!?"

Aaron saw the dead men in Cortez's room. "Cortez!"

"I'm here Aaron."

"What happened? Where's Luna?"

"They took her."

Aaron shoves Cortez up against the wall. "How could you let this happen!? You've never let your guard down!"

Aaron continues to yell when he notices the passion marks on Cortez's neck.

"Cortez, what is that on your neck?"

Cortez was silent. Aaron struggles to turn Cortez around.

"No, Aaron, wait!"

Aaron spots Luna's symbol on Cortez's back. Aaron's eyes widen as he stares at Cortez. He steps back in disbelief.

"Cortez. Did you, did you sleep with Luna?"

"Listen, I can explain."

Before Cortez could get another word out Aaron throws a dagger at his head. Cortez quickly dodges and stares at Aaron with surprise.

“Are you crazy Aaron!? That almost killed me!”

“That was the point! I left you to protect Luna. Instead, you were busy sleeping with her while I fend for my life in the forest!”

Cortez frowns at Aaron. He walks over and kicks him forcefully into the wall.

“Yeah, I did. I didn’t just sleep with her. I made love to her all night.”

“What! You bastard!”

Aaron chases Cortez to the dining area and lands a punch to his face. Cortez picks him up and slams him through the table. Aaron coughs trying to catch his breath. Cortez stands over him. He was about to stomp down when Aaron suddenly kicks him in the stomach. Aaron gets up and wrestles with Cortez until they fall to the floor. Aaron mounts on Cortez and continuously punches him in the face. Cortez throws him off, in return he mounts Aaron and continuously punches his face. Aaron, with all his strength pushes Cortez off him. Both men get back to their feet and grabs their weapons.

“I trusted you, Cortez! You were like a brother to me!”

Both men clash their weapons knocking them from their hands.

“What do you mean? We are brothers!”

They land a punch so hard on each other that it knocks them both to the ground. They both lay back on the wall trying to catch their breath.

"Please Aaron, listen to me. I will never in my life try to hurt you. You are my family bro. You, Miquel, and Marcel were the only family I've ever had. You guys never rejected me like the rest of the world. The moment I met Luna my heart felt warm. She didn't see me as weird. She was the only woman who ever loved me. I never thought I would find love. I need her, I love her. So please, I beg you. Don't stop being my bro. I love you man."

Aaron's heart felt pain when he saw the tears flowing from Cortez's eyes. All the years knowing him, growing up with him, he has always shown a happy and goofy side. This is the first time he's ever seen Cortez so vulnerable. Aaron had overlooked how the people treated Cortez due to his positive attitude. He never once considered how he truly felt inside.

Aaron painfully walks over and sits next to Cortez. They rest their heads on each other and exhale.

"I will never stop being your brother Cortez. You also mean a lot to me. It's just that Luna already had Miquel and me. I got scared and didn't think about your feelings. You were always there when I needed you most. I'm glad you have someone who loves you. You never showed us how painful life was for you. So, I'm here for you. You are family and I love you bro."

Both Cortez and Aaron were startled from the clapping at the entrance of the dining area.

"How sweet you two. Looks like you two really made a mess here."

Cortez and Aarons heart drops. They didn't hear Miquel ever entering the yacht. He was the last person they wanted to anger with the news of Luna. Aarons words stumble as he speaks.

"Miquel, h-how long have you been standing there?"

"Not long. Just enough to see you two beat the heck out of each other."

"How did you find our location?"

"Do you really have to ask? You were my apprentice, Cortez. You know I could track anyone if I wanted to."

"Oh, yeah. I forgot how scary you could be."

"Why are you both trembling? Doesn't matter, so, where is Luna. I'm surprised my love hasn't stopped the two of you. She doesn't tolerate violence very well."

"Uhhh." Both men say.

Miquel makes his way over to heal them both when he notices the dead bodies. He growls with anger at the sight.

"Cortez, Aaron! Where is my wife!?"

"The assassins took her." Cortez says.

Miquel grabs both men by the throat and holds them off the ground. "Explain!"

Aaron struggles to speak as Miquel squeezes tighter. "It was Cortez's fault. He was looking after her and got distracted."

"What do you mean, distracted?"

"Well, if you stop choking us, we can explain it to you better." Cortez says.

Miquel drops them to their feet. They both cough as they gasp for air.

"Now, tell me what happened."

Cortez was about to explain when Aaron interrupts.

"Cortez was distracted by Luna and let her get abducted. He made love to her and now he's her husband too."

"So, you didn't think Luna would get close to Cortez? What did you do, leave her with him?"

Aaron looks nervously at Miquel. He glances over at Cortez who had a grin on his face. Aaron immediately hated Cortez at that moment.

"Uh, yeah, I kind of did. Multiple times matter of fact."

Miquel rolls his eyes. "Idiot. So, Cortez you have Luna's symbol of love on your back, correct?"

"Yes, I fell in love with her. You're not mad, are you?"

"No, I knew you would fall for her the moment you two met. I'm glad you finally found someone to love you. A bond is for life and is a symbol of your love for each other."

"Wait, you're not mad at him?"

"Of course not, Aaron. What I'm mad about is that you let your guard down Cortez. Even when your making love you should always stay alert, you idiot."

Cortez twiddles his fingers and pouts. "Sorry boss. She just felt so amazing. I've never felt pleasure like that before."

Both Miquel and Aaron exhaled and thought for a moment.

"She does feel amazing." Miquel says.

"Yeah, we understand what you mean Cortez."

"Well, I understand that was your first time with Luna. She can throw you off your game. For now, we need to focus. I will heal the two of you so we can go rescue our wife."

Aaron was concerned. "Miquel, what if Marcel kills her. We must hurry before he takes his anger out on her."

Miquel let out a laugh at Aaron's words. "If I know my brother, which I do extremely well, he won't kill her. In fact, we should hurry before something else happens with her."

"Yeah, we need to rescue her before we go rescue August."

"Oh yeah Cortez, I totally forgot about him in the Twisted Forest. I wonder if he escaped the clan."

"So, the both of you left August to fend for himself against the clan?"

Miquel set out a stressful sigh. "You idiots. Have you lost your touch or something. You better hope he's still alive."

CHAPTER 19

UNDERGROUND CAVE

Underneath the ground of the platform was August wandering lost. He worries that the other two would never find his location.

"Where am I? I've been wandering around in this cave forever. If it wasn't for these blue glow crystals, I wouldn't be able to see what's ahead of me. It's like a maze down here. I don't even know if I'm heading in the right direction. Oh wait. What's that? And opening? I can see light."

Augusts runs to the giant hole where the light was coming. His eyes widened from the sight of what he was seeing. There in front of him was an underground world full of trees and shadow creatures. August could see plenty of food to eat from the plants and trees. There was water for him to drink from the waterfall that flows into a clear river.

"What is this place? I feel like I stumbled across a new platform world or something. This underground land is massive. Even though there's no moons down here, there is plenty of light from the purple crystals above. Let's see if there is a way out of here. There, I see something. There is another opening on the other side of the cave. I should study the layout and make my way there.

After studying the lands, August begins his journey through the cave world. He grabs some berries to eat and drink his fill of water for the journey ahead. August had been walking for hours until he spots a house in the distance.

"A house! Someone might be living down here. They might help me find a way out."

August sprints to the door and knocks on it. "Hello! Anyone home!?"

He turns the knob to see that the door was unlocked. He quietly peeks inside to find that no one has lived there for quite some time. August was wowed by the sight of the inside. It was a little dusty but still was nice enough to live in. He sees it was filled with expensive furniture and carpet inside.

"Wow, this place is pretty nice. I wonder who it belonged to. I should look around. I'm still wet and need something dry to wear. It's freezing down here, and I don't want to die from the cold."

Augusts opens the closet door in one of the rooms. "Men's clothes? I guess there were men living down here at one point in time. Lucky for me, now I have warm clothes until mines dry off. I need to see if whoever lived here had a map of this cave. This place was well surrounded by food and water. Whoever they were must have something of use. They picked a secure spot for survival. If I can't find anything, then I will just have to survive until I figure out this place."

August walks around until he feels the ground rumble underneath him. He runs to the window and peeks out the curtain to see that the trees were shaking. There emerging from the trees was a mountain size shadow. Augusts falls to the floor with his back up against the wall. He covers his mouth not wanting the creature to notice his presence.

The massive creature let out a loud screech that echoes through the cave. August was frightened. He peeks out the window moving as slow as possible. He couldn't make out what the creature could be. The only thing he knew was that it was larger than the trees and with every step the ground shook.

"This is all Luna's fault." He says in his mind. "If she hadn't invited me to this dangerous platform none of this would have happened. No, now is not the time to be blaming people. I came here because I wanted to. Because I wanted Luna. But… Aaron is still around. I feel like I never had a chance with her anyway. I hope I can make it back to her alive and ask her what's really going on here. That is if she is safe. Until I see her, I'm going to have to make it out of here alive but with that thing out there, I have less of a chance."

CHAPTER 20

UNEXPECTED MEETING

August didn't know that Luna had been taken by the assassins. She was locked away in her cell with her hands and feet chained to the wall. Luna barely can see what was in front of her due to the dim lighting of the dungeon.

Two men were guarding her constantly pouring cold water over her body.

"Oh, look at her nipples. They're getting hard." The assassin man says.

"Yeah, she's pretty hot too. We should have our way with her. The boss will probably kill her anyway." The second assassin says.

Luna watches as the men laugh as they plot to have sex with her. "Please don't touch me. I'm already taken and bonded."

"So, what's that supposed to mean?" The first assassin says. "You can't do anything to stop us."

Luna screams as the two men approach her. Thrown from the shadows was two daggers aimed straight at the men's head. They both fall dead at Luna's feet.

"My apologies, my dear." A hooded man says from the shadows. "I wouldn't have hired scum like them if I'd known they rape women."

"You're their leader?"

"I am. Now, let's get you free. I told these idiots to bring you straight to me not lock you up. (Sighs...) Good help is so hard to find these days."

Luna couldn't help noticing the hooded man staring at her wet body.

"Sorry for staring. I've never seen a woman quite as sexy as you are before. I thought only Royals were allowed to look this beautiful."

"Thank you for the compliment."

"My pleasure. Now, let's get you out of those wet clothes and into something dry. You can follow me to my private floor. You will be safe there."

"I don't know this guy's true motives. I should do what he says and be careful around him. His voice sounds just like Miquel which makes me feel safe around him. I can see he even has the same hair length as Miquel seeing that it flows down to his knees. Well, this is his brother so I guess that's why his voice and image would be similar."

Luna follows the man down the long dark narrow hallways until they reach his private floor. He opens the door and gestures for her to walk in. She pauses by the luxury of his private area. The bedroom she entered was fancy with chandeliers and soft red carpeting. The room was like a small home with a kitchen, bathing room, and living area.

"The bathing room is to your right. I will hand you a pair of clothes to change into."

"Thank you, sir." she says softly.

Luna walks away to the bathing room.

"She does have nice manners." He says softly. "How the heck did Aaron snag such a beautiful woman like her. Does she even know he's an assassin? I'm going to have to ask her these things when she comes out of the shower. I'm so distracted by her. I'm trying my best not to stare at her amazing body. Seeing her wet made it easy to spot those perfect breasts through her shirt. Her scent as well is driving me crazy. Something seems strange about her. She smells like a Queen, but not. It's strange. I can't help but feel like she belongs with me. What the heck is going on?"

He watches as Luna enter the bathing room. She steps into the shower and lets the warm water run down her curvy body. There, she thinks of what she can do to get out of her situation.

"Miquel's brother. He doesn't seem like a cruel person like Aaron and Cortez described. Maybe he's tricking me so I can give him information about Aaron. I don't know what to make of all of this. I can't escape this place with him and all his men surrounding the area. Miquel and the others say he's very skilled. So, I guess he would catch me even if I tried."

Outside the room Miquel's brother was still thinking.

"What is wrong with me? I can't get her beauty and body out of my head. Those curves, her round ass. Plus, her voice is so sweet and gentle. I feel the need to protect her. I want her so bad. I can't be forceful though. She needs to feel comfortable so I can question her. Maybe I'll take this cloak off so she can trust me more."

He removes his cloak and leans up against the wall waiting for Luna. When Luna steps out of the bathing room her eyes widen with excitement.

"Miquel!"

"Wait, what?"

Before he knew it Luna was already kissing him passionately. He couldn't help but kiss her back and feel on her ass and body.

"Oh, my love, I knew you would rescue me. How did you know I was here? When I heard your voice, I didn't think it was actually you. I missed you so much. We have to hurry before your brother Marcel arrives."

"Wait I thought this was Aaron's wife." he says in his mind. "Did those stupid men grab my brother's wife? Damn it! He's going to kill me. Looks like we have the same taste. This is definitely the woman I would have fell for as well."

Marcel looks silently into Luna's eyes.

"Miquel, what's wrong love?"

"I'm sorry to disappoint you, my dear. But I am not Miquel. I'm his twin brother Marcel. I'm glad I got a chance to meet his beautiful wife."

Luna immediately becomes embarrassed by her actions.

"I-I'm so sorry. Miquel never told me he was a twin."

Marcel let out a laugh. "That's just like him. Always playing mind games to see how things play out. I'm sorry I put you through this. I wasn't after you, my dear. I was trying to get a hold of Someone else's wife."

"Who Aaron?"

"Uh, yes, how did you know?"

"Well, um, I am also his wife."

"What?"

Marcel stares down at Luna. "Well, I didn't expect to hear that bit of news. Do you mind if I check your back to confirm what you're saying."

"Sure. As long as you don't hurt me."

"I wouldn't do that, my dear. Trust me, my brother would rip me apart before he dies if I did that."

Luna couldn't help feeling an attraction to Marcel. She knows he looks like her husband, but his attitude charmed her. Marcel reads her body language as she stares at him. He knew she was attracted to him as he was to her. They smile at one another as she turns to show him her back.

Marcel was surprised to see that Luna had three bonding symbols of love on her back.

"Luna was your name, right?"

"Yes, that is my name."

"I see that there isn't two but three symbols on your back. May I ask who does the third belong to?"

"His name is Cortez."

"Cor..! Cortez! This woman is something else. What are the odds she's married to all three. It's not like they hit and quit her. These symbols prove their love for one another. Ugh, it makes me jealous. How dare they share such a beautiful woman and not think to invite me. I'm going to kick their ass when I see them again. There's no doubt they will come for her. By that time, it will be too late."

"Are you okay, Marcel? You have a sinister look on your face."

"Oh, it's nothing. Luna, would you mind sitting with me for a moment?"

"Sure, I don't mind. What's on your mind?"

"I'm sure you know that we are all assassins."

"Yes, I'm aware of that."

"Then you must know that I must kill Aaron."

"Wait, please don't!"

"You will be fine Luna; you have two other husbands, so you won't die okay."

"That's not the point Marcel."

Luna places her hand gently on his cheek and stares into his eyes. "Marcel, there is more to the story about your sister. Miquel told me how much you both loved her. I know that Aaron wouldn't kill and innocent woman. He wouldn't want to hurt you or Miquel. Trust me, don't you think Miquel would have already killed him? If you don't believe me then at least let Aaron explain his side of the story. You raised him, so if anyone could tell if he's lying it would be you."

Luna's words spoke directly into Marcels heart. He has had mixed feelings about the situation this whole time. He becomes even more attracted to Luna at that moment. He stares down at her soft lips as she stares at his. Luna's body becomes nervous as she has seen Miquel look at her in the same way Marcel was doing.

"Luna, I feel very attracted to you. I know you feel the same. This feeling isn't something I take lightly. You are truly special. I hope you feel the same."

"I do. I know this might sound strange, but I always get this feeling in my heart when I find someone special. I am getting that from you just like my other husbands."

"It's not strange at all. For the first time ever, I know I want to bond with someone. That someone is you, Luna. Will you bond with me and be my mate and love for life."

"Yes, I will love to bond with you."

"I'm happy to hear that. If you don't mind, may you kiss me like you did before? Minus calling me Miquel of course."

Luna lets out a laugh at his silly joke. "Yes, I can kiss you like that. Maybe even better. Just make sure you touch me like you did before."

"Oh, I can do even more than that, Luna."

CHAPTER 21

THE 4TH HUSBAND

Marcel leans in to gently kiss her lips. Luna's sweet kiss satisfies his craving to kiss her once more. He grips her hair as their kiss intensifies. Luna climbs on top of him as he begins to rub all over her body. He lifts her dress and rips her panties apart.

"Oh my." she says in her mind. "He's so aggressive with me as well. I love it. How do I keep getting lucky enough to find these attractive men. This may seem like I'm going too fast, but I feel the need to bond with him as well. My body doesn't know how to react to him."

Marcel feels Luna's body begin to tremble. "Hmm, it looks like you already know who owns you, Luna. Do you like it when I take control?"

"Yes, I love that." she whispers.

"Well, if that's what you want, then I will show you who's in charge."

Marcel places Luna on her hands and knees. "Arch your back Luna."

Luna didn't know what to expect of him. She decides to listen to his demand anyway. "Yes, sir."

"You better not move or else."

"Hah, yes. Whatever you say."

Marcel kneels and firmly wraps his arms around her thighs. He begins to lick her pussy from behind.

"Hah, wait Marcel. That feels way too good."

Luna moves her body forward as she tries to handle Marcel's head.

"I thought I told you not to move."

Marcel forcefully pulls her back to him and licks and kiss her pussy more aggressively. Luna screams his name repeatedly as he kisses and bites her ass and nibbles on her pussy. She bites her bottom lip trying to handle the pleasure she feels. Marcel rises to his feet after he is done eating her.

"Now, Luna, it's your turn to show me what you can do."

Luna tries to recover from the feeling he gave her. She catches her breath to speak. "I will gladly give more pleasure than you gave me."

"Ha, is that so? Then show me."

Luna gently pushes Marcel to lay back on the couch while she gets on her knees beside him. She unbuttons his pants and lower them. Marcel rubs her hair as she leans down to suck him slowly. She goes deeper on him causing him to moan slightly.

"Hah, damn, Luna. This feels amazing."

Marcel rubs her back down to her pussy and begin playing with her. She moans as she continues to suck him.

"Hah, Marcel. I want you inside me."

"Then do something about it."

"Hah, yes sir."

Luna was becoming more nervous by the way Marcel looked at her. She climbs on top and sits down on his hard penis.

"Mmm, Luna, you are so wet and juicy. Your pussy feels amazing."

"You turn me on Marcel. I love how you take charge of me."

"Is that so, then I order you to ride me now."

"Hah, yes. As you wish."

Luna leans forward and kisses Marcel as she rides him. He holds her tight around her waist as she bounces on top of him. Marcel tries to hold his composure as she satisfies him. He grips her ass digging his nails deep into her. Luna turns around and reverse rides him. Marcel bit down on his bottom lip as he watches her plump ass bounce on him.

"This woman is driving me crazy." He says in his mind. "Makes me angry that they hid her from me. There is something special about her. She must be a Queen. I will investigate that later. I'm enjoying the way she feels right now."

Marcel, feeling angry, positions Luna to where her hands rest on the head rest of the couch. She leans forward as she prepares for Marcel. He pushes deep inside her and pounds her from behind. He places his hand around her mouth as she moans loudly and whispers in her ear.

"You love the way I pound you, Luna?"

Luna muffles, "Yes" under his hand. He grips the back of her neck and continues to dominate her.

"Hah, Luna, I want more of you."

He picks her up allowing her to wrap her legs around his waist. She holds him tight as he kisses and thrusts inside of her. Luna's body started to shake the longer he went.

"Hah, Ah! Marcel! Please stop! Please stop."

Marcel continues, until he releases deep inside her. His grip tightens around her as his body tenses. They both exhale and smile at the pleasure they received from each other. Luna and Marcels symbols of bonding love forms on their backs.

"That felt incredible Marcel."

"I have to agree. You felt unbelievably satisfying."

"I felt your symbol form on my back Marcel. You really did want to bond with me as I wanted to with you."

"Yes, I felt yours as well. You are mines now, Luna.

"Yes, I am."

"That also explains some theories I was having as well. I will need to discuss that with Miquel when I see him."

"What theories? Is something the matter Marcel?"

"Not at all my love. I will explain some other time. Until then, how about we take a bath together Luna."

"I would love that."

The two of them make their way to the bathing room and cuddle in the warm water together.

"So, tell me a little about yourself Luna. I must know more about my new wife."

"Well, I am a Noble born who's able to have multiple mates and have royal children. I already have three children, one being Aaron's and the other two belonging to Miquel. I am friends, well, more like sisters, with the Queen of my home world. She takes care of my Royal born children so they may grow to marry her Royal born children."

"That sounds amazing. I always wanted Royal children. And you say you are Noble born? Who told you that?"

"Miquel did."

"Ha, he did huh. What a liar. There he goes again with his games."

"What do you mean?"

"You are not a Noble born Luna."

"Marcel, I don't like secrets. Would you care to explain."

"Well, that's the thing. It's hard to explain. Let's just say you are closer to a Royal born."

"What, impossible! I don't have powers nor does my eyes glow."

"I'm telling you the truth my dear. Your powers are within you. I can't awaken them."

"But… Royals can only bond with Royals. How do you explain all of the bonds I have with you guys?"

"You are different Luna. I don't know how but you can bond with whoever you like. Please keep this a secret for now. I will explain it to the others later. Well, not Miquel, I'm sure he knew this already. He may have kept it a secret to protect you from other men. He might be researching for an answer as well."

"Thanks for telling me this Marcel. I'm glad I can bond with such wonderful men. I knew something was strange by the way I felt when I met all of you. I felt fated to be with all of you."

"I felt it too. That's why I want to know more about it. We are together for life now so don't worry about a thing."

"I won't. You are amazing, you know. Maybe someday we will have our own children."

"I will look forward to that day, Luna. I love you."

"I love you too Marcel."

CHAPTER 22

LUNA'S RESCUE

Marcel wakes up the next morning with Luna snuggled on his chest. He thought how her warm naked body felt good against his own. He pulls her so he can kiss her neck gently.

"Mmm, Marcel that feels good."

"I hope it does. I was about to take a shower then fix us a morning meal."

"You mind if I join you in that shower you're about to take?"

"I don't mind as long as I can make love to you once more."

Luna giggles at his words. "Of course, you can. Just go easy on me this time."

"I can't promise that Luna."

Luna and Marcel start their day unaware that Miquel, Aaron, and Cortez were making their way to the hideout.

"Miquel, what's the plan?"

"Don't worry about it just yet Aaron. You will soon find out. It may seem risky, but I know my brother quite well."

Cortez was curious about what Miquel had up his sleeve. "What do you mean Miquel?"

"Just wait until we get there, you'll see."

The three of them quickly jump through the forest until they spot the hideout. Inside Luna and Marcel had just finished eating their meal when there was a knock at the door.

"Boss. I have summoned everyone for our meeting today. They have all returned from their mission sir. We will wait for your arrival."

"Good. Have them wait. I will be down soon. If anyone tries to leave before I arrive, then have them killed on the spot. I have no tolerance for disobedience."

"Yes sir boss."

"I apologies for that interruption Luna. I always have my meetings in the morning."

"It's no problem. But I am curious. What does your clan do? Do you hurt innocent people?"

"Ha, goodness no. We hunt tyrants. That is how me and my brother intended it to be. When he left it felt like the clanmates lost their way. We hire new members rarely. New ones come in hurting and raping others. I usually have them taken care of right away. I don't like people like that. Makes me sick. When we discover a tyrant, we gather all the people of the lands and warp them to safety secretly. Then we take out the tyrant. That way no one dies. The mission will only go that way if my members follow the rules carefully. Lately, they have been nothing but failures. I may have to disband the clan one day if these failed events keep happening."

"I understand now. I'm relieved to hear that is the assassin's job. This whole time I thought you guys hurt people. Now that I have that information, I will wait for you when you return."

"Well, I'm not leaving yet. I have some time before I make my way to the bottom floor."

Marcel grabs Luna and kisses her. "So that gives me more time to be here with you my dear."

Marcel was unaware that his brother, Aaron, and Cortez had arrived. Aaron and Cortez waited in the tree while Miquel went off into the forest.

"Aaron it's been a while. Where do you suppose Miquel went?"

"I don't know Cortez. He gave us orders to wait here until he returns."

"This spot is kind of far from the hideout though."

"I don't know what Miquel is planning Cortez. We just have to wait."

Suddenly the ground rumbles, almost knocking Aaron and Cortez off their feet.

"Aaron, what the heck's going on? Did the Queen die or something?"

"No, or the platform would be breaking apart. This is something else."

Miquel makes his way back to them jumping quickly through the trees.

"Miquel! What did you do!?"

"Oh, you'll see Aaron."

Inside the assassin's hideout Luna and Marcel can feel the rumble as well.

"Marcel, what's going on?"

"I know this feeling! Luna, hurry! Run to the window now!"

Luna didn't hesitate to follow his orders. Marcel quickly grabs his belongings and heads towards the window. He places Luna on his back and throws his rope to the trees. He quickly jumps and swings on to the branches as far away from the hideout as possible. Luna looks back to see a giant shadow bull emerging from the trees. This wasn't any ordinary shadow bull. He was named "Legendary Giant King Shadow Bull". The king bull was larger than the hideout. It runs at full speed toward the building, crashing into it. The bull crumbles the building like paper, killing everyone inside.

"Oh, my goodness Marcel! That's the legendary bull I read stories about. He destroyed that building like it was nothing."

Jumping from the shadows onto the same tree as Marcel and Luna, was her husbands.

"Miquel, Aaron, Cortez! You're here!"

Miquel gives her a pleasant smile. "Of course we are Love."

"Yeah, so you can hand over Luna, Marcel."

"I'm not handing over my wife Cortez." he says as he glares at them.

"Your wife! Luna!" The men shout.

Miquel couldn't help but tease his wife at that moment. "Luna, we didn't take that long."

"I, I can explain. Um, well, what happened was."

They all try not to laugh as Luna struggles to explain her case.

"Luna, we're going to have to put a leash on you woman."

Luna becomes nervous as she speaks to Miquel. "He's the last one okay."

"Sure, he is." The three of them say.

"Look Miquel, this is all your fault. You didn't tell me you were a twin."

"Luna just because he looks like me doesn't mean make him your husband. I know I can be quite irresistible to you, so I get it."

Luna gives him a shy smile knowing that he was right. She knew her husband likes to mess with her when she becomes nervous.

"Miquel! How dare the three of you try and keep her for yourselves!"

"We would have told you eventually brother."

"Oh, really, and did you do this? What if you had killed Luna and I in that building!?"

"Oh brother, stop being so dramatic. I knew you would still be in your room. You never change your schedule you know. As for Luna, well you are my brother, I knew you would find her attractive. You bonded with her kind of fast, but it all worked out as plan, right."

"You asshole."

Miquel let out a laugh. "So, Luna, how did you react to seeing Marcel for the first time? Did you think he was me? Or did my brother trick you into sleeping with him?"

"I'll kick your ass for saying that brother. I don't need your help to fall in love with Luna. And yes, she did think I was you and kissed the heck out of me."

Miquel continues to laugh at his brother. "I love seeing how things play out. What are the odds that Luna be with the four of us."

"Yeah, we are family. I wouldn't have it any other way. But your predictions can be a bit scary depending on how accurate you are Miquel." Cortez states.

"It's the same with your feelings you have Cortez."

"Oh, I never thought of it in that way. I guess you have a point."

Marcel frowns at Miquel. "Your mind was always dangerous brother."

"You are a danger in your own way too brother. That's why no one would dare to challenge us."

"Uh, guys. I hate to interrupt, but what are we going to do about the bull?" He just spotted us."

"Aaron is right. He's looking right at us. Can I tame him?" Cortez says with a cheerful grin.

"No!" The men shout.

"You crazy animal lover." Marcel says.

"Marcel, hand Luna over to Cortez. We all know how he feels about killing animals. I need you and Aaron to help me take down the bull."

"No brother. I'm not working with Aaron. We can do this ourselves."

"Marcel, please listen to me. You know I would never do anything to hurt you or Miquel."

"Will you two save this conversation for later. That bull is about to charge any minute now. The three of us need to work together. Cortez, get Luna far away from here!"

Luna quickly kisses all her men and hops on Cortez's back.

"You guys better not die."

"We won't." The men say.

Cortez jumps far away from their location. The three men look nervously at each other.

Miquel looks over to Marcel and Aaron with a nervous smile. "We may die."

Both Aaron and Marcel nod their heads. "Yeah, I agree."

CHAPTER 23

BULL FIGHT

"What's your plan Miquel?"

"It's simple Aaron. When the bull charges we will jump on its back and kill it."

"Miquel! We don't have time for your games. You know it's not going to be that simple."

"Oh, being dramatic again Marcel? We got this. Now, get ready because the bull is heading straight for us."

The bull's sturdy body was easily bursting through the trees as it charges towards them. The forest shatters into pieces as the bull rampages at maximum speed. When the bull was close enough to their location the three of them jumped onto its back. They wedge their weapons into its hide as the bull continues to run.

"Hang on tight you two!" Miquel says. "He's going to try and buck us off!"

The bull becomes enraged, bucking and crashing into the surrounding trees.

"Marcel hand me your sword now!"

"What? No brother, this is my favorite sword."

"Would you rather Luna and the rest of us die because you favor a piece of steel?"

Marcel frowns at his brother. His logic was correct about the situation. He reaches behind his back and hands Miquel is weapon.

Miquel searches for the beast's weak spot. "This should be the spot."

Before he was about to stab the beast, he suddenly loses his balance from the bull's rapid movements. "This bull doesn't like us right now. I never seen him so angry before."

Miquel gains his footing once more. He looks over his shoulder and sees Marcel lose his balance and fall off the side. "No! Brother!"

Aaron quickly grabs a hold of Marcel before he could fall to his death. He wedges his dagger into the bull's side barely hanging on to the piece of steel. Marcel thinks in his mind as he stares up at Aaron.

"I don't understand. Why would he save me? Was Luna right about the situation? Is there more to the story about my sister's death? Aaron could have just let me die and be done with me."

Aaron and Marcel climb back onto the bull and wait for Miquel. He was busy trying to find the right area to kill the bull. He locates the spot and stabs the bull in the back of the neck. The bull let out a loud roar as Miquel dragged the sword down its spine slicing it clean open. The platform shakes as it falls dead to the ground.

"You did it Miquel!"

Marcel looks suspiciously at Miquel. "Of course he did it Aaron. Brother, did you even need our help?"

"Of course not. I just wanted some company. Fighting a shadow bull of this size can be scary you know."

Aaron's joy vanishes after hearing Miquel's words. "Why do you toy with us?"

"It entertains me." he says jumping down from the bull.

Luna runs from the forest to meet up with them. She grabs and kisses them one after another.

"You crazy men! You could have been killed!"

"Oh Luna, I know seeing us fight that bull aroused you." Miquel says as he grips her waist.

"Yeah, it kind of did." Luna says as she blushes. "It still doesn't give you an excuse to be reckless."

"That is true Luna."

Cortez falls to his knees near the face of the dead bull. "No, look at what you've done. You've slain such a beautiful shadow creature."

The men roll their eyes at Cortez's display.

Miquel couldn't help feeling bad for Cortez. He was the one who used it to his advantage. "Sorry, Cortez. We will let you tame the next creature we encounter."

"Promise?"

"Yes, we promise." Aaron says patting Cortez on the back.

As they stand over the body of the shadow bull, they realize the weather is changing. Thunder sounds off as the clouds become darker. The lightning begins to strike the ground not far from their position.

"We need to find cover fast."

"Not yet Miquel. Aaron, I need to settle some unfinish business with you."

"Marcel, wait. Don't do this my love."

"It's alright Luna. "I knew it would come to this. Marcel and I have to settle this."

CHAPTER 24

A FIGHT BETWEEN MEN

"Marcel, I need to talk with you."

"Not now, Miquel! This is between me and Aaron. Don't interrupt."

Miquel huffs and rolls his eyes at his brother.

"Miquel, Cortez, we have to stop them."

Miquel holds Luna close to comfort her. "It's no use in doing that, my love."

Cortez nods in agreement and comforts Luna as well. "Yep, once those two have made up their minds there's no turning back."

"They are just as stubborn as always. We'll just have to let them get it out of their system."

"Looks like the rain is starting Miquel. We should keep Luna dry."

"I agree. Luna, take our cloaks. It will keep you warm and dry."

"What about you two?"

Miquel smiles at her consideration. "We are used to this, Luna. We will be fine."

The rain starts to pour on Marcel and Aaron as they stare each other down.

"Marcel, I don't want to fight. I promise you. I didn't murder your sister. You know how I feel about family. I would never break the code."

"Enough talk Aaron. We will settle this the old way."

"Fine, if you won't listen, then I will make you listen."

The two men rushes each other and clash swords. They dodge one another's attack as if they mirrored each other.

"They move as if they can read each other's movement."

"Well Luna, that wouldn't be surprising. Marcel did personally trained Aaron. They have fought many times like this before." Miquel says.

"Really? Who won most of the time?"

Miquel was silent for a moment before he answered Luna. "Aaron has never bested Marcel Luna."

"Wait what!? Doesn't that mean?"

"Yes, Luna. Aaron will most likely lose this fight."

"No, he'll die. We have to stop this."

"They will be fine, Luna. Just watch and see."

Luna watches as her husbands continue to fight. Aaron tries to dodge Marcel's attack but instead gets his arm sliced. Aaron ignores the pain and focuses on Marcel's movements. He knows he will die instantly if he takes his eyes away from him. They continue the fight as the storm rages above. The two men knocks their weapons from each other's hands and begin to fight with their fist.

"Give up, Aaron! You can't beat me."

"I'll just have to try then!"

The storm intensifies as they resume their fight. Marcel manages to trip Aaron causing him to fall backwards. Marcel kicks him in the stomach while he tries to get back to his feet. He grabs his weapon from the ground and walks over to Aaron. Aaron quickly gets back to his feet dodging Marcels swings. Marcel swings until he finally slices Aaron on the side of his waist. Aaron let out a scream of agonizing pain from the deep wound. He falls to his knees and looks up at Marcel.

"Go ahead, Marcel. Kill me. But before you do just let me tell you that I still love you. You are like a second father to me. The four of us are like family. I will never harm my family."

Marcel looks into Aaron's eyes and knows he was telling the truth. His eyes water as he looks at Aarons sadden face. Marcel drops his weapon and reaches for Aaron. He holds him close to his heart as his tears fall.

"Damn it, Aaron. Why didn't you come talk to me. You know running like that made me suspicious of you. I know you wouldn't lie to me. I just want to know how my sister died. Look at what you made me do. Here, let me heal you."

Behind them, Miquel and Cortez claps with approval.

"Great fight you guys! Looks like Marcel won again!"

"Yes, that was very entertaining. Now that you two idiots are done fighting, I can explain what happened to our sister. First, Aaron was set up by Rocks. He secretly was in love with our sister. When she set off to marry her husband, Rocks became jealous. Apparently, he was also jealous of you and Aaron's father son bond. So, the asshole thought why not sabotage them both."

"Well, if Aaron didn't kill our sister, then who did?"

"Her husband was to blame brother."

"Impossible! Dragon Kings are extremely passionate about their wives and overprotective. They would never harm their Queen."

"I am aware of how their bond works brother. Her husband didn't try to kill her. He was aiming for Aaron who was only talking to her. He missed and stabbed our sister in the heart."

"Where's Rocks, brother! I shall kill him for what he has done!"

"There is no need for that brother. Rocks is dead. Cortez found him and brought him to me. He confessed everything to me while pleading for his pathetic life. Cortez and I had him torn limb from limb by shadow wolves. Every time he came close to dying, I would throw him a heal so his torture continued. Eventually, I let him be eaten. I don't understand how you don't know this already. Did you not read my letter?"

"Letter? I haven't heard from you in some time brother. I have never received your letter."

Miquel was confused. "I gave the letter to Cortez to deliver it to you."

"Oooh, I knew I forgot something. As a matter of fact, I have the letter right here in my pocket. Every time I try to deliver it, I would get distracted. That's why I keep bringing it with me. Ha, looks like I got distracted again."

Everyone, including Luna, had a look of shock on their faces.

"Cortez." Miquel says trying not to strangle Cortez. "You never.. delivered.. the letter?"

"No, I did try though."

"Miquel! You left a letter that important in the hands of Cortez! Do you know how long I've been in pain and out for revenge? Damn it, I almost killed Aaron!"

"I know, I know brother. Even I make mistakes sometimes."

"It's fine now, right?" Cortez says nervously. "We are all together again and we have Luna. Even though everyone in the clan is dead but it's fine."

"Well, that one was on me. I missed you brother, so I went on and had the bull kill everyone."

"What? You could of just visit brother, not have my whole building and men destroyed."

"I've done my research on those scums that you've hired brother. You don't need to surround yourself with trash, it will ruin your reputation."

Luna couldn't help but acknowledge her husband's way of thinking. "You are so cruel Miquel. Are you sure you are not the bad twin?"

"We are equally bad Luna, but not tyrants. That's why I had the clan destroyed. Plus, I think you like bad men. Look at you, falling in love with four assassins."

Luna frowns and blushes at Miquel's words. She hated it when he kept putting her feelings on the spot.

"Yeah, Luna is a naughty one. I don't regret having those idiots steal her and bring her to me. As for you Aaron, I'm done healing you now."

Once Marcel was done healing Aaron, he walks slowly over in Cortez's direction.

"Uh, M-Marcel? We're good, right?"

Marcel looks at Cortez with a fierce intimidating look. "Of course, we're good Cortez. My brother and I raised you like our own child. And, like a parent sometime your child must be punished."

"Wait, what are you going to do to me?"

"Nothing. I'm just going to give you a little love, tap!"

Marcel punches Cortez in the face knocking him unconscious.

"Marcel!"

"He will be fine Luna. I'll go heal him."

Aaron interrupts. "No Miquel don't heal him. He so deserved that punch."

CHAPTER 25

NIGHT IN THE FOREST

Luna and her husbands finally found a place to set up camp. The storm continues as they make a fire in the cave they found. Luna's husbands were soaking wet and had to strip off their clothes. They lay them by the fire to dry and sit down to warm themselves. Everyone waits patiently for Cortez to wake up. Luna had already stripped Cortez of his clothes so that he doesn't freeze in the damp cave. When Cortez finally wakes, he looks around with a puzzling look on his face. He studies his surroundings trying to figure out what was going on.

"Ugh.. What happened? Oh, wait, I remember now. Marcel punched me. You're so mean man."

"Cortez rambles on for a bit about Marcel's bad temper. They laugh as he complains and whines.

"I'm so glad everyone is happy with each other again. This must be how you guys were in the past. I'm glad I get to witness it." She says in a shy tone.

Her men smile at her shyness.

"We're glad you feel that way, my love." Miquel says.

"Oh, Cortez. Are you alright? You're shivering."

"Oh, I'm ok Luna. I'm just a little cold."

"Would you like for me to give you my clothes to cover up? I don't mind taking them off for you. My body stayed dry thanks to you and Miquel."

Miquel, Aaron, and Marcel became excited by Luna's generosity. They look at Cortez as he was given an opportunity to get Luna out of her clothes.

"Oh no Luna, it's fine. I wouldn't want you to be cold."

The men's faces drop when they hear Cortez response.

Miquel tries to help Cortez understand the situation. "Cortez. Are you sure you don't want to take Luna's clothes?"

"No, no. I'm good."

Miquel turns his head to the side and laughs. He couldn't hold it in any longer. On the other side you could see the veins popping out of Marcel and Aaron's head from pure frustration.

"Cortez. You shouldn't be cold. You should... take Luna's offer." Marcel says squeezing his teeth together.

"Really, guys, I'm okay."

Miquel's laugh becomes contagious causing Marcel and Aaron to join him. The men shake their head with disappointment. Even Luna catches on to what her men was trying to do. She gives him the offer once more as she tries to hold in her laugh.

"Cortez, I will be totally naked if you take my clothes."

Everyone waits silently in the cave as they stare at Cortez. They waited until he finally catches on.

"Oh, oooh. Yes. Luna, I'm so cold. I am freezing right now. I'm going to need all of your clothes."

Cortez gives the men a wink and a thumbs up. "Her clothes will be off in no time guys." he whispers.

Marcel shakes his head with disappointment as he jokes with Cortez. "Something's seriously wrong with you Cortez."

They all enjoy that funny moment together as they wait out the storm.

"It's fine Cortez. I will gladly give you, my clothes."

The cave becomes silent as they watch Luna slowly strip off her clothing. Their mouths water at the sight of her naked curvy body. She then throws her clothes to the side and mounts on top of Cortez.

"They say body heat is better for warmth." she says seductively.

Her husband becomes jealous, wanting the same treatment.

Aaron speaks first. "I'm cold Luna!"

Soon after, Miquel joins in. "I'm freezing."

"Luna, I may die from how cold I am."

"Don't you think that was a bit overkill brother?"

"Yes, but I don't care Miquel."

Luna chuckles at her men. "Why don't we all cuddle together. This cloak is dry so snuggle up with me."

Aaron looks around and thinks about what Luna was suggesting. "Uh, Luna. Two of us will be snuggled next to the other."

"Ew, I don't need their naked bodies touching me." Marcel says.

"Guys, grow up and choose who's going to be next to me." Luna says crossing her arms.

"I will be next to you for sure."

Luna smiles at Miquel as he takes her hand.

"Then I'll be the other.

"No Aaron, I will be next to her."

"No way Marcel! You just became her husband and should be on the end."

"Come again Aaron!" he says with a serious look on his face. "You want to fight me for that spot instead?"

"Uh, you know what, I think I'll take the end."

They all lean against the wall and snuggle up together.

"Luna, would you mind telling us about how your life was growing up?"

“Sure Cortez, but... it’s not the best childhood. I wouldn’t want to bore you with my past.”

“It’s fine Luna. We don’t mind listening.”

“Thank you, Aaron. Well ok, where do I start. I grew up in my village with the most perfect parents anyone could ever ask for. They would spoil me with their love and affection every day. The people of my village spirits were lifted every time they came around. Helping others always brought my parents’ joy. Eve, before she was known as a Royal, was my best friend. She was still living happily with both her parents at the time. We would play and sleep at each other’s houses. I never cared why she never revealed her face. All I cared about was how kind she was to me and everyone in the village.

One day her mother was discovered which changed everything. The royal guards came to take Eve’s mother to the Dragon King to be married. Our village was spared thanks to the rules. Eve’s mother moved to a different platform since our world was already claimed by Eve’s husband. I never understood the pain she felt that day. I would catch her crying alone everyday as she missed her mother. Eve, nor did her father, would show the people of the village how they felt about their broken family. They continued to smile and help others. I always thought of how brave they were to deal with such pain. I knew that one day her father would die from heartbreak. My parents would also worry for him. They wanted to ease his pain as much as possible.

One day they decided to pick him flowers and make a special gift for him. They set off to the Illusion Woods to find the perfect set of flowers. That was the day my life changed for the worse. My parents never returned from their journey that day. The villagers knocked on my door with urgency. When I opened it, I could see their faces drenched with tears. They handed me my mother's necklace and my father's pocket watch. The two items were covered with blood. The people of my village told me that they were killed by a pack of savage shadow wolves."

Luna pauses her story as she begins to cry. Her past brought up feelings that she wasn't expecting. Her husbands hold her close as they rub her back. Luna feels the comfort of her men and continues her story.

"So, after that day, I would stay in my home and cry to myself. The villagers would feed me and make clothes for me to wear. One day Eve's father showed up at my door. He asked if I wanted to live with him and Eve so that he may raise both of us as sisters."

Miquel admired the man's actions. "That was very kind of him Luna."

"So, that explains why you two are so close."

"Yes, that's true Aaron. Eve's father's kindness is why we are closer than ever. You know living with them wasn't bad. He treated me as if I was his own daughter. All of us would cry about our lives but would quickly support one another's needs."

Luna exhales for a moment and looks to the ceiling of the cave.

"The next part of my past was a little annoying to remember. Days after Eve had her mother taken and me losing my parents, a boy and his family had recently moved to the village. They were well dressed and seemed a bit stuck up. This boy was a brat that always bragged about his parents and the things they had."

Aaron rolls his eyes. "That must be August you are speaking about."

"Yep. August at a young age was a real pain. I had enough of his bragging one day. I told him how selfish and inconsiderate he was. I didn't speak to him for weeks until one day he showed up with flowers and apologized for his actions. After that day, he never bragged in front of me nor Eve again. We all grew together as friends as we got older. Some days I would still see him as annoying but never showed my feelings in front of him."

Luna smiles slightly. "You know he saved my life in the woods years ago."

"Really? That guy saved you?"

Luna giggles. "Yes Cortez, it's hard to believe but he did. He was so brave that day. I was attracted to his bravery until one day we had a bad fight. I had a mission from Eve that I had to fulfill, and August refused to journey with me. He said the people's lives didn't' matter to him. I slapped him and I went to journey alone through the woods."

"I remember that day very well."

"Yes, I met Aaron in the woods who also saved my life. Seems like I keep getting into trouble. I was grateful to be saved from that shadow wolf. I also didn't mind you taking advantage of me either."

"Aaron!" The men shout.

"W-Wait, guys. She wanted it too."

Luna laughs at Aaron's nervousness. "I'm only joking guys. I was very much attracted to Aaron just like I was with all of you."

Luna's husbands squinted their eyes at Aaron in suspicion.

"Guys, cut it out. All of you had the same feelings for Luna as I did."

Marcel sighs. "Yeah, I guess you have a point. Go on Luna continue your story."

"Sure. So, you all know that I got pregnant by the assassin August hired which made me hate him again. I was happy I met Aaron but hated that August would do something so cruel. Everyone including my child would have died if the King was killed. I knew Aaron wouldn't' go through with it. Even so, he was still locked away for his actions as well as August. Not long after Miquel and I became close and fell in love. He was the only man who was honest and loving. He filled the hole in my heart after Aaron was separated from me. We had two beautiful children of our own and planned to get Aaron out of prison. I slipped Aaron the key to his cell but never expected him to return back to me."

"I would have done everything in my power to return back to you Luna."

Luna smiles as she looks over to him. "I knew you would Aaron."

"If it wasn't for you and Miquel I probably would be locked away as we speak. They are probably still searching for me."

"Not exactly. When I went back to research some details, I came across Queen Eve. She told me to tell Luna that if Aaron steps foot on their world he will be captured. Until then, he is a free man."

"Eve said that!?"

The tears fell down her cheek as she felt the love her sister as given her. Eve was always so kind to me. To do this for our family means the world to me. I will always love her."

"She is truly a magnificent Queen."

"Yeah Miquel, I agree too. She's the reason why her husband hasn't killed me you know."

"I'm happy to hear that. I didn't know she stopped her husband for you. You know what, I don't mind the way things turned out. I was able to bond with four sexy men because of it. I wouldn't trade you guys for anything."

"Awwww, Luna." The men say hugging and kissing her. "We love you."

"I love you guys too."

"Luna, I love the way you are. You are so kind, and you accepted me for who I am, red hair and all."

"Yes, you never judge us for our ways either. Even though I'm the last to meet you I'm glad things turned out the way they did."

Aaron reaches over and holds Luna's hand. "I have to agree with Marcel. You gave us the love we've been waiting for."

"Oh, you guys are making me blush. We should… Woah, what was that? I, I feel dizzy all of a sudden."

Miquel become concern. "Luna, are you alright?"

Luna suddenly faints and falls over to Marcel.

Her men all shout her name as they try to wake her.

"Luna! Luna!"

CHAPTER 26

HOME AGAIN

Luna, after 30 minutes of unconsciousness, finally wakes up to find her husbands watching over her.

"Wah... what happened? Did I pass out or something?"

"Yes, you did Luna. I'll explain later. For now, I need you to eat these plants for me."

"Why do I need to eat Miquel?"

"Just eat it woman."

"Oh, ok. You know I like it when you tell me what to do Miquel."

Miquel tries not to blush as he smiles at her.

"Wow, these plants taste good. I'm feeling better as well. What are these plants?"

Cortez was overjoyed to hear that Luna liked the plants. "They are Pink Sparkle Berries and Twisted Roots. I went out and picked them myself."

"Thank you love. They taste amazing. I guess I was just hungry or something."

"No Luna. That's not the case actually. You see, you are pregnant."

Luna looks at Miquel with excitement. "Really! That's wonderful but. I slept with Cortez and Marcel around the same time. Who's the father?"

"Well, that's the thing. Marcel and I were trying to figure out what we discovered. You are pregnant with twins. One child belongs to Cortez and the other belong to Marcel."

"Miquel." She says with a giggle. "Stop joking around."

"He's actually telling the truth love. I confirmed it myself. Both Cortez and I are the father."

Luna's eyes widen at Marcel's words. She couldn't believe something like that was possible. She gives a shy smile as she looks down at her food.

"Awww, Luna. You are happy about the news, aren't you?"

"I am Cortez. I get to carry both of your babies at the same time. I can say that I'm the mother of all my loving husbands' children. My boys back home are going to be so excited when they hear about this, and that the family has grown. And Eve. Oh gosh, Eve. Once she hears I can have babies in this way she's going to go crazy. There's no doubt she will want me to have more babies. Miquel we should go in to hiding."

Miquel and the others laugh.

"No, my love. Looks like we will just have to keep making babies for her."

"I guess you're right Miquel. Whatever I am must be the cause of all these miracles."

"What do you mean my love?"

Luna looks over to Marcel. "Well, Marcel said I'm not a Noble born. I'm more like a Royal born. Is that true Miquel?"

The men all look to one another in silence. Miquel felt it was time to explain the situation further.

"My Love. All of us discussed this while you were passed out. I didn't want to scare you about your body. You are a Royal born but your powers are broken. You are like a cross between Royal, Noble and Common born. I've have been trying to figure this out for years. I was going to tell you as soon as I came up with a solution or answer. You have the ability to bond with whoever you like. I'm sorry for hiding this from you all these years."

"Wow, um, so much information at once. I didn't know I was born that way. I guess it doesn't matter. I bonded with all of you and that makes me happy. Though, I wish I could use my powers."

"We will find a way to figure that out my dear."

"Thank you, Marcel. So much excitement. I can't wait to see where the future takes us." Luna says as she giggles.

"I know, this is all great news to me. Let's keep getting Luna pregnant guys."

They all laugh at Cortez's statement. As they all laugh and enjoy their moment with Luna, Aaron was thinking of a plan.

"Hey, guys. Come over here and talk with me for a second."

The men huddle up in a circle and whisper to one another.

"Guys, do you think Luna can carry all of our babies at once?"

"Marcel and I were just discussing that, Aaron. We believe it's possible. Marcel and I have come up with a theory on how we think it works. I'm sure Luna is the only woman that is capable of doing this. This may even spread to our future children as well. I'm getting excited just thinking of the history we're making."

"When she gives birth to the twins, we will experiment this theory." Marcel says.

"What are you guys whispering about?"

The men were startled by Luna as she snuck up behind them.

"Luna, that was great! No one's ever able to sneak up on us like that. You training to be an assassin or something?" Cortez asks in a joking matter.

"Well, Miquel has taught me some things over the years. But the answer is no. I'm not cut out for what you guys do. As for today all of you are retired from this assassin business. You have responsibilities now."

"Well, all my men are dead anyway thanks to my brother over here. Shouldn't be a problem quitting now. I am excited about being a father and husband."

Miquel gives his brother a slap on the back and smiles. "I am happy for you and Cortez, brother. Becoming a father is amazing. But we should get back to Cortez's house. The rain has let up and Luna needs as much rest as possible. Carrying twins is hard on the mother's body."

Miquel was coming up with a plan on how to take care of Luna. Him and the others were so focused that they didn't realize the shadow wolf sneaking into the cave.

"Guys, look out!"

Luna quickly grabs one of Aaron's daggers and throws it through the wolf's head. Her men clap and smiles at her skills.

Cortez grabs Luna and squeezes her tight. "Good job Luna!"

"Look at you, throwing like a pro. Did Miquel teach you that while I was locked away?"

"I think you would have made a fine assassin my love. I would have been proud to have and assassin wife by my side."

Luna becomes shy from her husbands' praise. "You guys, stop that. It was a lucky shot."

"No Luna. We have been training for years. That was all you."

Luna starts to blush as her men spoke. She loves how they treat her. It brought warmth to her heart the more she spent time with them.

"I think we've had enough camping for one day. We should get moving. We have a long journey back."

The men agree with Miquel and begin packing their belongings. They travel through the Twisted Forest for miles until they reach Cortez's Mansion. When they step inside, they all exhale with relief.

"We made it. That was quite the adventure we had."

"That's kind of how our life is all the time Luna."

The men nod their heads in agreement with Cortez's statement.

"Well, I'm exhausted. A day in you guys' shoes is enough for me. I'm going to take a hot shower and bath and get out of these clothes. Wait, Marcel. What about you? Your building was destroyed along with all of your belongings."

"Worry not Luna. That was just my hideout. My real home is hidden not far from here."

"That's a relief to hear. Will you guys have food ready when I get out of the bath? I can really use some meat to eat right now."

"No Luna!"

Cortez pulls her towards him by the waist and rubs her belly. "I don't want our babies, eating meat."

"But Cortez, I'm so hungry. What else can possibly fill me up?"

Miquel, Marcel, and Aaron roll their eyes as they knew how passionate Cortez was about not eating the shadow creatures.

"Here we go again." The three of them say.

Aaron leans up against the wall and shakes his head. "She doesn't know what she started."

"Luna! There are so many other options! I will gladly make you a healthy dish and prove to you that you don't need meat to feel satisfied. Well, unless it's mine of course."

"Cortez!" The others shout.

"What? You guys know it's true. She likes our meat."

Luna let out a laugh at Cortez's statement. "He's right you know. But let's get back to the food subject ok love."

"I hate to admit it, but Cortez's cooking is amazing."

Miquel and Aaron both agree with Marcel. He knew how to make anything taste good.

"Well, I will give it a try for you Cortez. I will see you after my bath."

Cortez turns around and grins at the others.

Aaron panics knowing the familiar look in Cortez's eyes. "Oh, no, what do you want Cortez?"

"Nothing much, just for all of you to help me pick the ingredients from my farm."

Miquel huffs at the thought. "Cortez, no. Your farm is huge."

"Pleeeease, for Luna."

"Fine, let's go then. You and your annoying pouty face."

CHAPTER 27

HONEST FEELINGS

Miquel, Marcel, Aaron, and Cortez did their routine scouting of the mansion and outside area. Even though the other assassins were dead they always stayed alert. It was a habit of theirs from long ago. Once they finished, they headed over to the fields after confirming that Luna was safe. The men look around seeing how much work Cortez has put into his farm over the years.

"Goodness Cortez, there are even more shadow creatures here than the last time I visited."

"Well, you know me Marcel, you know how much I love the different creatures I run across. Especially the rare ones."

"Yes, we know." The men say in a monotone voice.

"Guys not to change the subject but we need to talk about August."

"Oh, yeah, I keep forgetting about him Aaron. I hate that guy."

Marcel was surprised at Cortez's statement. "What? There is someone out there that you disapprove of. Wonderful! We can hate him together. That guy was just as Luna described.

Spoiled little brat. If I had known he wasn't your little brother Aaron, I would have let the men kill him."

"I met him back at the Palace. My job as the Palace doctor also includes examining the prisoners to make sure they haven't harmed themselves. He was indeed spoiled as if someone's supposed to treat him differently."

"So that brings me to an important question. Do we still want to search for this guy? I personally don't want to leave Luna to give birth alone or with someone else."

The men nod with agreement at Aaron's words. Neither wanted to risk leaving their wife.

Miquel rubs is chin thinking of a solution. "If we do decide to search for him it would have to be after Luna has the babies. I personally want to help Luna through birthing her first set of twins."

"I think he's already dead to be honest. Last time we saw Augusts was when he was running from the members of the clan after Aaron and I split up."

"I don't think he's dead Cortez. Well, not by the hands of the clan. My men reported that they lost him in the forest. I had those idiots killed for not being able to capture a guy like August. It wouldn't have been fair for them to live after they failed. The other assassins died at least trying to capture you and Cortez."

"I guess you have proof on that matter Marcel. If the creatures haven't killed him already then he might still be alive. What do you think Miquel?"

"My theory is that he is still alive Cortez. He must have gotten lost or something. Either way, he's going to have to wait until Luna gives birth. She comes first."

"How will we explain our plan to Luna Miquel? This guy is her friend even if we don't like the bastard."

"Just leave it to me brother. I know how to talk to her about these sorts of things."

"Guys, I think we have everything we need for our meal tonight. Come with me to grab a bag of rice and we can finish this conversation at home."

"Good, because I'm starving." Aaron says rubbing his stomach.

***

The men travel back to the mansion and lay the ingredients out for Cortez. They gather at the table and continue to talk while Cortez prepares the food. Luna walks in smelling the meal and fresh bread being made.

"Hey there love. Did you enjoy your bath?"

"Yes, I sure did Miquel, it was needed. My body feels so relaxed right now. I also can't wait to eat this meal Cortez is cooking."

"Well, actually it's done now. You can have a seat Luna and I will serve you."

Cortez places the food on the table of vegetables curry, freshly baked veggie bread, and desserts from plants that Luna has never seen before.

"Eat up Luna, I know the babies must be hungry."

Luna tastes the food and smiles with satisfaction.

"Cortez, I could kiss you right now. This food is so delicious. Mmm... and this bread is so warm and soft. This bread melts in my mouth. I feel great after eating just a few bites. If I eat these types of dishes everyday there would be no need to eat meat again."

"Really! Oh Luna, you are perfect. I will teach you everything about how to prepare these meals."

Everyone was enjoying the meal Cortez had prepared. When they finished, they all helped clean the table and dishes. Miquel suggests that Luna sits back at the table so they can discuss their feelings. Her men sit back at the table with a serious look on their face.

"Um, am I in trouble or something?"

"No, my love. We need to talk with you about August."

Luna's face becomes serious as a hint of sadness wash over her. "He's dead, isn't he Miquel?"

"We are not sure. I believe he is still alive, lost somewhere. This platform can be quite confusing if you don't know the lands very well. That wasn't the only reason we wanted to have this talk. You see, none of us wants to search for August while you are pregnant. We all want to ask you this serious question. This world is full of dangerous creatures and obstacles. If we were to die searching for August, would you be okay with that? Even if just one of us was to die?"

Marcel places his hand over hers. "If he is that important to you Luna, then we will search for him without judging your decision."

Luna's heart begins to race from hearing her men's words. She starts to feel pain in her chest as she thinks about the possibility of losing her husbands.

"No." she whispers. "Searching for August isn't worth it if I lose any of you in the process."

She looks to her husbands with a sad expression. "I can't lose any of you. I love all of you. August has been my friend for a long time, but I'm not bonded to him. If I was bonded to him then it would be different. I hate to say this, but his life is not more important than you guys' lives. So please… don't go."

The room was silent for a moment. The men smile and nod at one another.

"We'll find him Luna."

"Wait, Miquel no! I said you guys didn't have to go."

Aaron shrugs his shoulders. "Yeah, we know. We just wanted to know how you really felt about the situation and the possibilities."

Marcel nods after taking a sip from his cup. "We see that you will gladly choose us over August. That satisfies us, well, me personally."

"Now that we know how much you care, we can search for him when the babies are born. I have to be here for my little one's birth.

"Yeah, I want you and Marcel here for that as well. But, what about the dangers you guys mentioned?"

"Oh, Luna, we have been through and seen every bit of danger. Plus, this is our home, and we know it well. Even Cortez can confirm my words."

"Yeah, Miquel is right. We've went up against Dragon Kings and rare creatures. We will be fine. Searching and looking for clues is something we're good at as well. That's pretty much our job."

"That's a relief to hear." Luna says putting her hand over her heart. "If this is the plan, then I will send a message to Eve's mother when the babies are born. I'm sure she will help me with her grandchildren while August is being searched for. Are you ok with that idea Miquel?"

"That sounds like a good idea love. Now, we wait for these little ones to arrive."

CHAPTER 28

NIGHT BEFORE THE RESCUE

Four months had passed since Luna became pregnant. Today was the day she finally was going to give birth to her twin babies. Her men take the time to prepare the room. Her men stand beside her bed supporting her.

"Miquel, I can feel the baby. Hurry!"

Miguel sits at the base of her and prepares for the first child to be born.

"Luna, I need you to breathe just like we've worked on and push."

Luna controls her breathing and begins pushing out the first child. He was a Royal born with red hair and dark grey horns on his head. His face was peaceful with a gentle smile on his face.

Aaron smiles at the child. "Well, we know who he belongs to."

Cortez burst into tears as he gently held his first child. He gives him a soft kiss on his forehead. "He's beautiful. May I name him Luna?"

"Of course you can Cortez."

"I will give him the last name of the one who helped bring our family together. I shall name him, Cyrus Lotus."

Miquel approves of the honor Cortez has given him. "Aww, Cortez I'm touched. Thank you for that."

"Ah! I hate to interrupt but I believe the second baby is coming!"

"Luna's right. The second one is ready. I must help her."

Marcel waits anxiously as his son is being born.

Luna pushes and gives birth to another Royal born with white hair and dark grey horns on his head. He had a frown on his face and his eyes glowed fiercely when he cried.

"Why is he so angry?"

"I agree with Cortez, he looks like he's going to kill someone."

"Well Aaron, he is my son after all. He's probably mad for having to share a womb with Cortez's son."

"Heyy… That's mean." Cortez says in a whiny voice.

They all share a laugh as Marcel tease Cortez. He gently holds his son and kisses him on the forehead.

"He is also beautiful." Marcel says as his tears begin to fall down his face. "I wish my sister could have been here to meet him."

"She would have loved our children, brother. What name do you think she would have liked?"

"I wish to name him Miguel. Miguel Lotus."

Miquel let out a small chuckle. "Wow, now we have two boys named Miguel. We really do think alike."

"Are you saying your son's name is Miguel, brother? You make me so angry sometimes ya know."

Luna giggles at her men. "It's okay Marcel. I'm okay with having two sons named Miguel. I will love every child all of you give to me no matter what their names are."

They smile at Luna's sweet words. Cortez and Marcel hand Luna the babies so that she may nurse them.

***

A few months later, Luna and her babies where ready to journey over to Eve's mother's Palace. The men made sure that the children were safely in Queen Leona's care before returning home with Luna. They all sit at the table after returning from the Palace. They want to discuss how they were going to go search for August.

"Okay, now that we have taken care of the babies, we should discuss how we are going to prepare for this mission. There will be no splitting up. We will stay as a group as we search for clues to see if August is still alive. Luna insists we take her with us, so our top priority is to keep her safe. We will leave in a few days."

Miquel looks at the men in a way they could understand. They had no intentions of ever taking Luna with them. They had other plans for her instead as well as keeping her out of danger. Miquel gives the signal for Cortez to start their plan.

"So, um Luna. I want to ask you something."

"Yes, of course Love."

"So, can we hit that before we leave? We haven't had you in months and I think we could concentrate better if we did."

"Absolutely Cortez! You think you guys were the only ones who's been wanting to make love."

"Well, you know all of us would like to have you at once Luna. Do you mind if that happens?"

Luna becomes shy for a moment after Miquel's suggestion. Thinking of having all of them at the same time made her nervous, but she didn't want to pass up the opportunity.

"Y-Yeah, I wouldn't mind." she says softly.

The four of them escort Luna to the bedroom and surround her. Luna instantly becomes nervous which made her breathing flutter.

"Don't be nervous." Miquel whispers into her ear.

Marcel whispers in her other ear. "We don't bite. Well, maybe a little."

Cortez gently massages her body. "Just relax and let us please you."

"We'll take great care of you." Aaron says as he kisses down her thighs.

Luna's body becomes hot as her men feels and rub all over her body. All she thinks about is how sexy they were and how amazing they are. Miquel and Marcel suck and kiss her neck while Cortez and Aaron lick her nipples.

"H-Hah, guys wait. I don't think I can handle this. But I do love it."

"We know you do Luna." Miquel says.

Luna continues to moan as they strip her clothes and kiss down her body. They lay her back onto the bed and begin rubbing her juicy pussy. Marcel enjoys how her body reacts.

"Well, well, well, look who's already wet down there."

Luna's nerves were getting the best of her. Her body was shaking as the men continues to tease her. Miquel lowers himself down her body.

"How about a little taste."

"Yeah, I haven't eaten all day. I think I'll join in as well."

Both Miquel and Cortez went down to lick and suck all over her pussy. At the same time Marcel and Aaron were sucking her breast making her moan loudly. Her men switch positions taking turns pleasing her.

"Hah, you guys! This feels amazing! Let me have a turn, please."

She gets on her knees taking turns sucking and stroking their penis. The men moan as she pleases them. Miquel was the first to receive her head.

"Hah, Luna amazing as always. Let us feel more."

They lay her flat on the bed as they take turns laying between her thighs.

"Ah yes. I love how you guys are doing me."

They switch between different positions as they pound Luna more aggressively. She moans a scream as they continue to drive her crazy. Miquel picks her up and holds her as he thrusts inside of her.

"Ah, yes Miquel. You're the best."

Her men frown at her words as she looks over to them.

"Wait, all of you are the best." she says nervously. "It just a habit for me to say that to him you know."

Miquel chuckles and grins at Luna's explanation. "You don't have to explain Luna. You know I'm the best."

"Stop it, Miquel." she whispers. "You trying to get me in trouble?"

"Well of course. Now, let's continue."

Miquel finishes his turn and hands her off to Cortez. He lays on his back and allows Luna to ride.

"Ah Cortez! You are so big!"

Once again, her men frown at her words.

Marcel frowns and pulls her over to him. "That's it. We are about to make you pay for your words Luna."

Her men make love to her all night until they finish inside her. Luna takes a breath as she lays beside them on the bed.

"What has gotten into you guys? That was amazing. I felt a different vibe from all of you. Not to mention how well you guys work together. It was almost like you were communicating with each other or something."

"That's because we've been around each other for a long time Luna."

Cortez catches his breath as he speaks. "Yeah, I agree with Aaron."

"Well, we should all get as much rest as possible. We will be leaving for our mission soon."

Before Miquel says more, he looks over to see Luna had already fallen asleep.

Cortez chuckles. "Well, I guess that was a job well done. Let's hope our plan worked."

CHAPTER 29

NEW PLAN

A few days have passed since Luna's steamy night with her husbands. Her men were cooking and preparing a special meal for her before they supposedly set off for their mission. Luna joins them as they set the table for her.

"Wow, this looks wonderful! These are all my favorite dishes. Cortez, did you prepare all of this? What's the occasion?"

"Oh, nothing. I just wanted to make a special meal for the woman I love."

"Ok, now I'm suspicious. What happen?"

Aaron rolls his eyes. "Goodness Cortez, you are terrible at this."

"Hey, I'm trying okay."

Luna squints her eyes at the two of them.

"Hey there love." Miquel says softly as he rubs her back. "Do you mind if Marcel and I check something with your body?"

Luna had a confused expression on her face. "I guess."

Miquel and Marcel hover their glowing green hands over Luna's belly. They both smile when they receive their answer.

"It worked!" They both say with excitement.

"It worked!?" Aaron and Cortez say jumping from their seats.

"What worked? You guys better tell me what's going on."

"My love, please don't be mad at us. We couldn't help ourselves. We just got you pregnant with all four of our children. Marcel and I thought it might work, and it did."

"What! We were supposed to go search for August today, Miquel! Now that I'm pregnant, I'll have to wait another four months!"

"We had to know if your body was capable of doing this Luna."

"I understand Aaron, but couldn't your stupid experiment wait until after we find August. Damn it, he's going to die if he isn't already."

"Luna, calm down. You will strain yourself and the babies. We will still go search for August he will just have to survive a little while longer. Heck he might be okay and back at the main kingdom for all we know."

"What if you're wrong Miquel?"

"My dear, I'm hardly ever wrong."

"Except when you gave Cortez that letter." Marcel mumbles under his breath.

"Brother you need to let that go. It was a small mistake. To be honest we should be thanking Cortez's way of thinking. If he hadn't made that mistake, we wouldn't have met Luna and given her all of our children."

"Thanks Miquel. But I don't know rather to be happy or hurt from you guys' conversation."

"Don't worry, we all know how you can be Cortez." Aaron says wrapping his arm around Cortez's neck. "We all love you man."

"Aww, thanks bro."

"Guys enough jokes, what are we going to do now, seriously?"

"Luna, I've already notified Queen Eve's mother. She will be more than happy to help you take care of the babies when they are born. You will be staying there with Queen Eve who is also pregnant. I told them both that you are pregnant with all of our children. Queen Eve was so excited she insisted on staying at the Palace with you and her mother. She kind of spread the word about your pregnancy which made you the talk of the platforms."

"You told everyone before you could confirm it Miquel!?"

"Yes, I knew it would work. But love please, you need to relax."

"Fine I will calm down for now. All of you are going to be in trouble once I have these babies. On the other hand, Eve is pregnant again as well. I feel like she's doing this on purpose just so our kids can have mates. I shouldn't have told her that I was a Queen with broken powers. Now she's really going to want us to have babies."

Luna breathes in and exhales as she tries to take all the information in. She starts to laugh at how silly the situation has become. She especially laughs at Eve for being pregnant every time she was pregnant. She wanted to ease her pain from thinking of August.

"Well, I guess I'm okay with this. I get to spend more time with our other children. I will let you guys take over the mission while I'm with Eve and her mother. This might be for the best. I will only distract the four of you. I want you guys at your best while battling the dangers out there."

"We had hoped you understand, Luna."

"Oh, let me guess Miquel. This was a part of the plan to keep me out of danger while you also experiment?"

"You figured it out love. I had no intention of ever bringing you on our mission. It's far too dangerous."

"Look, I will be fine with this as long as you all promise me something important."

"What's that?" They all say.

"Don't die. All of you must come back alive, promise."

"We promise."

Her men share a hug with her as they feel her concern for their safety.

***

They went on to wait four more months until Luna gave birth to their four Royal born children. They placed Luna under the care of Eve and her mother and set off into the Twisted Forest.

Luna walks around the palace until she spots Eve.

"Luna, is something wrong?"

"(Sigh) Yeah, I guess you can say it is. Could you walk with me for a moment Eve?"

"Sure, what's on your mind?"

"So much is on my mind. I want my husbands to be safe on their journey, August is still missing, and now I'm a Queen with no powers. I don't know what to do with the situation."

"Luna, for one, your husbands will be safe, and as for August we both know he's alive out there somewhere."

"But the last time my husbands saw August he was being chased by assassins."

"Luna, do you feel in your heart that August would give up that easily? He's stubborn remember."

"I know, I feel like he is out there. If I hadn't..."

"Luna don't. Don't go blaming yourself for all that's happened. August is going to come back to us ok. Trust in your men's abilities, they will bring him back. I know it. Dr. Lotus is with them so don't worry about them being hurt, he's my head Doctor after all. I can't believe this whole time he had a twin who was also a strong healer as well. Cortez was it, is a tamer and knows the lands and you can't forget your assassin Aaron.

I'm really not worried, you have and amazing team of men Luna."

"Yeah… you're right. They are quite the team. It makes me smile just thinking of them."

"Let's talk about your powers. I can feel that they are in you. I feel that someone more powerful can help you with that."

"What about your mom?"

"No, I don't think she can help either."

"Hah, this sucks."

Eve giggles. "Hey, at least you know more about yourself. You have a gift. All these unique children you have, and you bonded with all the men you love is amazing. Just be patient, we will figure something out."

"Thanks Eve, I feel much better now. Let's go be with our kids. I will try and relax. I just hope my loves don't run into any trouble along the way."

CHAPTER 30

LOOKING FOR CLUES

"Ugh, Guys can't we just tell Luna that August is dead and be done with this? We've been out here for weeks without a clue to follow."

"No Aaron, we promise we will try for Luna. We need to at least confirm if he's dead or not. Can you imagine how angry Luna will be if we said he was dead then he shows up alive."

"Fine, I guess you're right Miquel."

"Don't worry Aaron. You're not the only one feeling this way. I miss my sons and could be with them right now. Instead, I'm searching for some idiot."

Cortez agrees with them but knows the job must be done correctly. "Guys, I feel the same as Marcel. But the quicker we find evidence the quicker we can return to our family."

Miquel knows all too well how the men where feeling. But as the leader he had to stay firm with their task.

"I feel the same as all of you but right now let's keep moving. We can't allow ourselves to let our guards down or miss something important."

The men agreed with Miquel. The four of them jump through the trees searching in the direction of the assassin's old hideout. They search for another full day with no results. They decide to stop and rest in a safe spot deep within the forest for a moment.

"Guys, I don't see any sign of August. What are your thoughts Marcel?"

"It's been almost a year since he went missing. I think Cortez is right, his tracks may be faint by now."

Aaron growls with anger. "Come on let's just be realistic. We all know a guy like him wouldn't be able to survive this long in the Twisted Forest. Let's just confirm it already and go home."

Miquel places his hand to his chin trying to analyze the situation. "Aaron, I understand your feelings but something else has been puzzling me. There is no sign of him even being dragged away or killed. It doesn't make since."

"Let's sit and think about it over a meal. Look I found some glow berries on the bushes over there. I'm sure we can all use something sweet right now."

"Yeah, you're right Cortez, I wish Luna was here. She can be my something sweet to eat."

Miquel couldn't help thinking of his wife at that moment. "I have to agree brother, that woman is just more than something sweet to eat."

They all joke and laugh until Miquel, Marcel, and Aaron pause with a shock expression on their face. Their eyes widen when they see what was behind Cortez.

"Cortez, move slowly and get up in the trees now." Miquel says in a low voice."

"Move now!" Marcel whispers.

The men move carefully up the top of the tree leaving Cortez on the ground.

"Are you guys joking or something?"

He looks back to see what was behind him. A glimmer of excitement was in his eyes as he had never seen a creature so beautiful before. Behind him was the Great Griffon of Legend. Its body glows a pure white with eyes sparkling a diamond pure blue. Its wings glow brightly as it reflects the full moon's light. The griffon's body stood about 12 feet tall and 6 feet wide as it stared down at Cortez.

"It's, it's beautiful."

"Cortez no! It will kill you!"

"No, yourself Miquel. You said I can tame the next creature we come across. I'm definitely taming this legendary beast."

The men sigh as they knew Cortez to well. Once he makes up his mind on taming a creature there's no stopping him.

"Don't die you idiot."

"I won't Aaron."

The men lay back on their trees and watch as Cortez readies himself to tame the beast.

"Hey, there boy." Cortez says in a gentle tone. "You know you don't have a choice but to be mines So, I will be taking you now."

The griffon let out a rebellious and loud screech as he circles with Cortez. Both circle each other never taking their eyes off one another. Cortez quickly finds an opening and throws his lasso around the griffon's neck. He pulls and holds on tight as the griffon flaps around and takes to the sky. Cortez holds on as he flies across the sky. He climbs the robe until he reaches the bird's head and mounts him. The griffon tries to buck Cortez off its back flying wildly in the sky. Before Cortez could react, he was flying up even higher at incredible speed.

Miquel, Marcel, and Aaron stop paying attention as they rest and eat their meal.

"He'll be back."

"Yep." Miquel and Aaron agree.

Moments later they hear a screeching sound coming back to the platform.

"Woo-hoo! I got him guys!"

They clap for Cortez as he achieves something magnificent.

"Guys, I'm going to fly around to find clues quicker. Stay here for a bit okay."

The men give him a thumbs up with approval.

Cortez flies around until he spots the underground cave.

"Oh no, that would explain why we couldn't find his tracks. I hope he's not in there or he may actually be dead. I have to report this to the others."

Cortez flies back and lands in front of the trees the men are in.

"Guys, you may want to come down here for a moment."

"What is it, Cortez? Did you spot something?"

"Uh, yeah, I kind of did Aaron. Let's just say this mission just got a lot more dangerous."

Marcel becomes impatient and snaps. "Just tell us what you saw Cortez!"

"I think August might have fallen into the Crystal Cave."

The men were silent after hearing Cortez.

Miquel could understand it may be possible. "We have to check and confirm."

They hop on the back of the griffon and fly to where the cave was. They confirm the tracks in which August was running and fell into the cave.

"Damn it! He must be dead! I'm not trying to die fighting that thing. Not for that guy. I know you agree with me Miquel."

"I agree with you brother. We could search for a bit. If we encounter that thing before we reach August, then we will leave him. Rather he's alive or dead, it's not worth it."

The men all agree.

Aaron looks to the sky with disappointment. "So, I guess we are doing this. What a pain."

CHAPTER 31

THE BLUE CRYSTAL CAVE

"Everyone, stay alert." Miquel whispers as they descend into the cave. "This opening is big enough for that creature to fit. If we're not focus it may cost us our lives."

"I understand, but can I at least take some of these blue crystals? I would love to make rings out of them for Luna an all of us."

"Yes, that's fine Cortez but make it quick."

"Thanks Miquel."

Cortez joyfully chisels away at the shiny blue crystals and places them in a small pouch. He joins the others as they approach the entrance to the underground world below.

"Well, it's just as beautiful as I remember. I wonder if our old home is still standing?"

Miquel's eyes widen with excitement. "Aaron you're a genius! We will search there. If August was lucky enough to make it there, then he may still be alive. There was always plenty of resources around there that could help him survive."

They all agree for them to start their search at their old home location. They ran quickly and quietly through the lands until they reached their destination. Marcel spots their old home in the distance.

"There, up ahead. It's still standing in one piece."

The men run up to the door and opens it. Out from the shadows, someone was swinging a bat uncontrollably at them. They dodge as they see it was August attacking them. Marcel becomes enraged and kicks him hard in the stomach. August falls back through the table groaning as he holds his stomach.

"Found him." Cortez states.

"Wah... it's you guys. Why are you guys here?"

Aaron frowns at his words. "You are unaware that this use to be our old home, you idiot."

"So, now what? You guys come to kill me?"

"No, or you would already be dead."

"Calm down Marcel. Luna sent us to search for you August."

"I don't get it. You are Eve's doctor and the one at the prison. Why would Luna be associated with all of you?"

Cortez was happy to answer August's question. "Well, that is because we are all her husbands."

"What? No, this, this is all your fault Aaron! You are to blame for everything that's happened. When I get out of here, I'm going to report that you escaped to Eve."

All the men roll their eyes at August's threat.

Miquel explains the situation to him. "You are an idiot. Aaron is a free man thanks to Queen Eve. You have been down here for almost a year, so you know nothing."

"Almost a year? That's it? I thought I was down here for much longer."

"No, you haven't. And will you stop blaming everyone else but yourself. Did you forget that this all started with you summoning the assassin to do your dirty work. Which happens to be false information. Eve's husband wasn't even a tyrant. I hate guys like you who will hurt others for his own personal reasons."

"Calm down Aaron. I can feel your rage escalating."

Aaron calms himself like Miquel says. His feelings about August were getting to him. August stands to his feet frowning at Aaron when the ground starts to rumble.

"Oh, no. Everyone get down now!"

They all drop to the floor like Miquel orders as they hear the giant beast circle around their home. The beast's shadow was large enough to cover their home in darkness. It let out a massive screech as it continues to walk away.

"Damn it! It's never been on this side of the cave before. Why is it so close?"

Miquel peeks out the window to see if the beast is still present. "I agree brother. I was hoping that we didn't have to encounter it while we are down here. We will never make it out alive if it's that close to our home."

"It comes around everyday around this time. I've been barely dodging its presence since I've been down here."

"That's not good. That means her nest is close by."

"Her, Cortez?"

"Yes Miquel, I've always known she was a female."

"She's a hybrid right Cortez?"

"Yes, but also a Legendary beast Aaron. The Giant Shadow Owl Bear. She guards the crystal cave that we are in."

"We have only seen her once before. She is known for being the most ferocious shadow creature on this platform. There is a law that forbids anyone from ever stepping into this cave. This entire area has been off limits because of her."

"That may be true Miquel. Some still enter but they never make it out alive. They want a chance to get the rare blue crystal from this cave. So dumb, they are always willing to die for them. I even had a few of my clan members try and make out with the crystals from this place. They are dead now, serves the bastards right for not following my orders to never step foot in this place. There are other dangers here than just that monster."

"Let's just hope we don't run into them as well brother. This cave is known to have creatures grow beyond their limits. They are all hybrids."

"You know guys, usually I would want to tame it but not this time." Cortez says shrugging his shoulders. "That beast is dangerous. Now that I'm a dad I don't' want it anywhere near my family."

Miquel, Marcel, and Aaron were all in shock by Cortez's words. Hearing him say that made them realize the dangers of this creature.

"Cortez, that was very mature of you to think that way. We would have to come up with a plan if we are to stop the owl bear and make it out alive."

The men all agree with Miquel and was preparing for their plan when August interrupts.

"So, Luna has a child with you as well?" He says softly.

"Luna has children by all of us August. That is why it's important we make it out of here alive. As her husbands, we promised to make it back to them. As leader of our team, I am to lead us all back safely. Even if we have to leave you behind.

"Wait. Please don't. I will follow your lead. I want to get out of here as well."

"Good." Cortez says cheerfully. "I'm glad you said that because we're going to need your help as well."

CHAPTER 32

CLOSE CALL

"Wah, what do you need me for?" August says nervously. "I'm not like you guys who probably use to doing this type of thing."

"Trust me, I have a job that even you can't screw up. Now, listen up guys. I spotted some blue oil trees not far from here. We need to get to those trees and cut the branches which holds the oil. This oil is highly flammable so be careful. Once that's done, we need to make torches and light them. Someone else will lure the shadow owl bear out so we can throw the oil on it and set it to flames."

"That sounds like a plan Cortez." Marcel says. "This isn't going to be a walk in the woods. We can all die if someone messes this up."

All the men stop and stares over at August.

"I won't mess up, okay."

"Good. Miquel, Marcel, I need you guys to gather the oil. Aaron and I will find what we need to make the torches."

"What do you want me to do?"

"I need you to be the bait August."

"What! No way! Are you trying to purposely get me killed? I won't do it."

ine, then you can stay here, and we can go home without you." Aaron says.

"Wait." August says softly. "I want to get out of here. I'll do it."

"Good, now that you and Aaron got that settled, let's continue. Cortez states. "I will have you stand in a designated spot so we can have a clear shot at setting this beast on fire. When you see it coming run straight and don't turn off until we do our part. Your job is very important. So, do it right, got it?

"Ok, I'll try my best." He says with an uneasy feeling.

The men split off into different directions to find what they need for the plan. They meet up in the spot Cortez told them to be moments later. The ground rumbles as the beast begins to approach. Ever thud of its footsteps rumbles through their bodies like thunder from above.

"It's coming!" Cortez says. "Hurry guys, get into position!"

August was trembling uncontrollably as he stood in his designated spot. He sees the shadow owl bear's glowing red eyes as it slowly approaches his location. The closer it got; the more August could make out its appearance. August observes its sharp black claws as it dug into the ground with every step. The blue wings looked like razers on the side of its thick muscled arms. The blue fur stood high on its back like a shaggy bush in the Twisted Forest.

August couldn't stand there any longer as his fear started to kick in. He dashes as quick as he can away from the raging monster.

"August wait! It's too soon!"

August ignores Cortez's warning. The shadow owl bear screeches when it sees August running. It begins to pick up speed as it chases August through the trees.

"I don't want to die! I don't want to die!"

August panic causes him to run circles right into Cortez's location. The beast slashes at the tree breaking it clean in half. Not making it out in time, Cortez was sliced in his side leaving a deep life-threatening wound."

"No! Cortez!"

Aaron swings and catches Cortez before he hits the ground.

Miquel, seeing the situation getting worse, knew he had to make the call. "Fall back, now!"

The shadow owl bear becomes confused by who to chase as the men split up into the trees. Seeing a glimpse of Marcel, it decides to chase after him. Miquel notices the beast changing in the direction his brother was running.

"Marcel she's going after you!"

"Damn, I knew it would come to this. Goodbye my favorite sword."

Marcel throws his sword straight into one of the owl bear's eyes causing it to stop its chase. The monster beast screeches loudly as it flails around in pain. The men run quickly back to the house and lays Cortez on the floor.

"I'm, I'm not going to make it guys."

Aarons heart pounds uncontrollably after Cortez said those words. "Shut up Cortez! You can't leave Luna and our family like this."

Miquel hurries to tend to Cortez's wound. He looks around for his brother's help.

"Marcel!"

"I'm here brother. We have to hurry and stop the bleeding."

Both brothers' hands glow as they begin slowly healing and closing the wound. Aaron couldn't control his rage as he sees his brother in the condition he was in. He looks over to August who stood far off in the corner.

"You asshole!" Aaron shouts aggressively. "You didn't think twice to follow Cortez's plan."

"Oh Yeah. Well, I didn't see you down there being bait for that monster. Your friend's plan was dumb to begin with."

Aaron rushes over and grabs August by the collar.

"What did you just say you cowardly scumbag?"

August frowns and pushes Aaron away from him. "You know what? I've had enough of you!"

August puts up his fist readying himself to fight Aaron. Miquel and Marcel were still healing Cortez. They couldn't help but glance over to see the situation.

"Are you trying to die, August?" Miquel asks.

"No. He's going too…"

Before August could finish, he had been punched in the face. Aaron then knees him in the stomach and throws him to the ground. He places his knees on August's arms pinning him in place. August was left helpless as Aaron continues to land punches to his face.

"You Scum! That's my brother you almost got killed! I don't see why Luna even cares for you! She told us we didn't have to search for you, but we did it anyway!"

"Aaron, stop." Marcel says quietly. "You're going to kill the bastard if you keep that up."

Aaron exhales as he understands Marcel's words. He walks over and falls to his knees over Cortez. He places his forehead on his as the tears fall from off his face.

"I love you bro. Please, hang in there. I can't go on without you. I don't care about this rescue anymore. Just be okay so we can go home to our family."

"Aww, that was so kind of you bro." He says softly.

"Cortez! Are you alright?"

"He's fine Aaron. This is a lot of work for Marcel and me, but we were able to stop the bleeding and close his wound. We are just healing the rest of his insides. Marcel and I are going to have to rest today and heal the scar in the morning."

"That's great news. That's all I needed to hear. I think I've had enough for one day."

CHAPTER 33

FINISHED BUSINESS

That night the men sat against the wall and rested. Cortez had already fallen asleep on Aaron's shoulder resting his sore body. The others glare over to where August was sitting with murderous intention in their eyes. August, feeling their vibe, tries not to make eye contact. He stays far away as he places a cold pack over his bruised face.

Aaron whispers to them. "We should kill him."

Marcel nods. "I wouldn't mind."

Miquel feels the same but had to think logically on the situation. "I could care less for his death as well. The only thing that's stopping me is Luna. We are here to bring back her idiot friend. I just want to get us out of here alive. For now, we will take turns resting. I don't trust this guy after what he's done."

Both Marcel and Aaron agree. They take turns watching each other's backs as they slept. The following day Cortez finally wakes up from a long night's rest.

"Hey bro. How do you feel?"

"Well, I feel a lot better Aaron, I'm alive thanks to you guys. I do still feel slightly drained of my strength so to speak."

Miquel was aware that Cortez would feel this way with his recovery. "Cortez your feelings are natural. It sometimes happens when a wound is life threatening. Marcel and I will give you some more healing. That will not only heal your scar but also recover your strength as well."

Cortez lays back and relax as the men begin to heal him. He let out a breath of relief when they were finally finished. "Wow! I feel great now!"

Before Cortez could say another word, he was grabbed by Miquel and holds him close to his heart. "I'm glad you are still with us Cortez. I can't imagine our life if you weren't around. Even though I have children of my own, I will always love you as if you were my own child."

Cortez's eyes water after hearing such strong words from Miquel. He couldn't hold back crying into his chest. "Thank you, Miquel. I know you care about me, but hearing you say that really brings joy to my heart."

Marcel tries to hold his tears in. He growls angrily. "Damn it, why is everyone doing this! I'm trying not to cry with all these emotions you guys keep having."

Aaron smiles. "It's okay Marcel. After seeing you cry that day let me know how much you really care for us."

Marcel snaps at Aaron's comment. "Shut up, Aaron! Don't you ever bring up my feelings. Of course, I care. I love all of my family but don't start thinking I'm going soft or something. I'll still kick your ass."

They all smile and laugh at Marcel. He was never good at showing his emotional side, but they could clearly see the love written all over his face.

Cortez starts to think. "Guys, let's try and kill the shadow owl bear again."

Aaron was concerned by Cortez's idea. "Cortez, no! I almost lost you already. I don't want to go through that again or worse."

"Well, this time it will be different. I won't leave our lives in the hands of an idiot this time. The four of us can do it. Just like the old days."

They all smile at Cortez's positive spirit and agree to go along with his plan.

"So, here's what I'm thinking. This time let's try and sneak back to the main entrance of the cave. I want the three of you waiting at the top with the oil and torches. I will be the bait this time."

"No Cortez!" They all shout.

August walks slowly over to the men. He overheard the plan to try again. "I will do it. It was my fault we failed the first time. If you all wait at the top, then nobody else will get hurt. I will run the owl bear to you guys."

Miquel raises an eyebrow at August. "You do understand that there's a high chance you can get killed. You're not as fast as a runner as the rest of us."

"I know, but you guys have family, right? I have no one to return to so it's best that I do it."

The men stare silently at August for a moment. They can see how serious he was about this plan.

Aaron frowns angrily. "Fine, just don't get yourself killed. We shouldn't have to explain to Luna that you volunteered to get yourself killed."

Miquel folds his arms and nods. "I agree with Aaron. Don't do anything reckless. Now let's hurry and get to the entrance."

The four of them run as quickly as they can to the front entrance. They feel the ground rumble after hearing the loud echo screech of the shadow owl bear.

Cortez climbs the rope quickly and warns the others with urgency. "Hurry guys! We have to make it to the top before she arrives."

August stays below until he was once again face to face with the beast. Their eyes met and August can see the owl bear's eyes was still bleeding. The aura from the beast was intimidating. She growls and lets out a raging screech at August. The wound that Marcel gave her was severely deep. It constantly gave her pain. Her steps pick up as she runs. August runs fast as the angry beast follows him. He was almost out of breath as he attempts to climb the robe to the top of the cave.

The men all shouts as August climbs. "Hurry August!"

The shadow owl bear barely sees August climbing. She let out another angry screech that tunneled through the opening of the cave. August ears felt as if it was going to burst from the loudness of her screech. The beast takes flight trying to reach August after he makes it to the top.

"Now guys!

They follow Cortez's orders and throw the oil and fire on the beast, setting it to flames. The beast flaps and screeches as it was being burned alive. In one last attempt the shadow owl bear goes after Cortez.

Aaron begins to panic. "No! Cortez, it's coming for you again!"

"She's not getting me this time Aaron." Cortez whistles loudly as he looks to the sky. Out from the clouds flies his legendary griffon. It swoops down in the blink of an eye and grabs Cortez by its feet. They fly quickly through the sky as the beast chases them.

Aaron looks to the others with concern. "What should we do!?"

Miquel reassures him. "There is nothing we can do but to trust in Cortez's ability. He will be alright."

They watch from below as Cortez pulls out his bow and arrow and sets it on fire. He shot dozens of arrows right in the chest of the beast. Not able to chase any longer, the beast's wings stop flapping as it falls towards the ground. It made a loud splash as it hit the water below. Cortez flies and lands at the shadow owl bear's face and couldn't help the feeling in his heart. The others run to his location and stop when they see the look on Cortez's face.

"Cortez, what are you doing?!"

Cortez ignores Aaron. He walks slowly to the shadow owl bear's face and rubs her. He looks into her eyes and sees the tears running down her face. She was in great pain but was still alive.

Cortez's heart aches. "I can feel you. Miquel, Marcel, please come here!"

The men run over to Cortez with confusion.

"What is it, Cortez?" Miquel asks.

"Can you both heal her? She doesn't deserve this."

Marcel snaps at Cortez's request. "Cortez, have you gone mad!? This thing is a monster. Plus, do you know how much effort that would take? Heck, this thing might kill us after we heal her."

"Please, trust me. I have a feeling we will be fine."

Marcel growls and frowns. "Damn it! I hate your feelings."

The two of them accepts Cortez reasoning and heals the beast. Soon after it stands to its feet and stares down at them. She lowers her head so Cortez can pet her.

Marcel shakes his head with disbelief. "You got to be kidding me."

Miquel smiles and chuckles at the occasion. "Cortez is truly gifted. He was right about his feelings once again."

The shadow owl bear rests on all four feet wanting Cortez to mount her.

"What is it girl? Is there something you want to show me?"

The beast let out a soft screech in reply to his answer. Cortez mounts her and takes flight back into the cave. The men wait patiently for Cortez's return. They begin to hear the massive wing flap as Cortez and the owl bear return.

"Hey guys look at this! She did have a nest like I predicted. That's why she was so protective of that area."

In Cortez's hand was a shimmery blue egg. The egg was as large as his body as he held it.

"I'm taking Blue back with us so she can hatch her egg in peace."

"Blue?!" The men say.

"Yep, that's the name I gave her. She can take you guys home while I take Sparkles to get Luna."

"Sparkles!?" The men say.

Cortez chuckles. "Yeah, that's the name of my Griffon."

Aaron was excited to ride on the back of the shadow owl bear. "I guess we better hurry and mount her so we can make it home before Cortez arrives with Luna. She's gonna be so surprised when she sees Cortez's new friends."

Miquel and Marcel agree with Aaron.

Marcel rolls his eyes. "Let's get this over with. I have never ridden something like this before. It better behave."

Miquel couldn't help but tease. He snickers quietly. "Are you afraid brother?"

"Shut up Miquel! I'm not afraid of riding this beast. It's just new to me that's all."

"If you say so. I will hold your hand if you need me to."

"I will fight you right here brother if you keep that up!"

Aaron laughs at their behavior. It brought back memories of their time together growing up. The men mount the beast. Hours later they finally returned home. They left Blue in the back of the land in the barn with her egg. Everyone waits patiently for Cortez and Luna's arrival.

Aaron sighs in relief "Well, we kept our promise to Luna. August is alive and safe. And we are all ok."

Miquel rests his elbows on the table and nods with agreement. "Yes, but right now all I care about is having Luna back in my arms. I hate being away from her like this."

Aaron and Marcel both agree.

CHAPTER 34

BACK TOGETHER AGAIN

Luna's husbands and August all wait at the table until Cortez returns with Luna. When she enters the room, she grabs and kisses all over them.

"Oh, my loves, you are all okay. I was so worried about all of you. Cortez told me everything about how things went with the griffon and shadow owl bear. I was extremely angry at myself when I heard Cortez almost died. I'm so sorry I let you all go out there."

Aaron rubs her back and reinsures her. "No, Luna. You've done nothing wrong. We volunteered remember. Even when you said we didn't have to go search for him."

"Oh, thank you my love for your kind words." Luna grabs her men again and continues to kiss them.

They were enjoying her soft lips after being away for some time. She looks across the room to see August standing there.

"August you're safe!"

She starts to walk toward him until she sees the look of disappointment on his face.

"August? What's wrong?"

"I see that it is true, Luna. You are married to these four men. I came here because you said I could be with you. Now I see you couldn't keep your legs close."

Luna gasp at August words. Her men become enrage but it was Miquel who reacts on the situation. He rushes over to August and punches him in the face knocking him back. He grabs ahold of his neck and chokes him until he was barely breathing. His blood was boiling with the aggression he felt. His protection over Luna was always his first priority. He leans closer to August's face while he chokes him. August can see the fangs and murderous intension in Miquel's eyes.

"Listen here you bratty asshole. I've kept my cool for the longest around you. We risk our lives to save you. Cortez, who is my family, almost died because of you! Luna has done nothing but worry about you this whole time. You were the one who left her on her journey alone. You got locked away for hiring an assassin. So don't you ever talk to my wife in that way again!"

Miquel drags August out the front door and throws him to the ground. "You stay away from my family! I better not see your face again unless you want to die. Have fun with this forest. If you die, it's not our problem. We did our job in bringing you back."

Miquel forcefully slams the door behind him and walks towards the others. They pat him on the back trying to calm his nerves. They look over to Luna seeing that she was crying to herself. They rush to her side to comfort her.

"Luna!"

"Was August right about me? I didn't just sleep with you guys you know. I felt love for all of you. It was a connection."

Miquel gently rests her head on his chest. "Luna, you are the kindest and most amazing woman I've ever met. August knows nothing about how strong our love is for each other. He has no idea that you are born different as well."

Aaron nods in agreement. "That guy has some serious problems. He only blames others. Don't take what he says to heart my love. You are a wonderful woman. I'm glad I got to beat the heck outta him when I had the chance. Bastard deserved it."

Cortez walks behind Luna and hugs her. "I know I fell in love with you the moment I met you Luna. I knew you were special. I will always love you just the way you are."

Marcel lifts her chin so she may look him in the eyes. "I as well fell for you at first sight Luna. To us, you were never someone we would just use and throw away. You didn't show us that you would use us either. That is why you are bonded to all of us, remember. We will be here to protect and love you always."

Luna wipes her tears and smiles at her men. "All of you always know just what to say to make me feel better. Hearing how you guys feel for me makes me happy. Right now, I know that I never want to see August again. He hurt my feelings."

Miquel understands her feelings. He smiles and holds her hand. "You don't have to, love. I don't think he will be returning after what he just did."

Luna was always grateful for how Miquel thought about her feelings. It brings joy to her heart at that moment. "Guys let's go to our room and cuddle. I haven't felt you guys' warm body for weeks. I'm not going to let what August said ruin our reunion."

Her husbands follow her to the bedroom. Luna lays on her bed as her men join her. They snuggle up with her as she slowly was drifting off to sleep. She was exhausted from the trip and taking care of all the new babies.

"I'm glad I have all of you. I never feel alone. I love you all."

Luna's husbands feel her love and appreciation as they watch her fall asleep. Her words always touched their hearts.

"Aaron."

"Yes, Cortez."

"I'm glad you took advantage of Luna that day."

"Damn it, Cortez! I didn't take advantage of her."

Marcel snickers. "What was the story again? You saved her then asks for the booty or something?"

They all laugh at Aaron as he frowns at Marcel and Cortez's comments.

Miquel enjoys the way they play around and joke with one another. He exhales and speaks softly as he was slowly drifting off to sleep. "Well, after a long line of events, we are family and will stick together forever."

CHAPTER 35

AUGUST'S REALIZATION

August, still lying in front of Cortez's home, thinks about all the things everyone had said to him. He listens, as the thunder crackled above his head and the rain starts to pour down rapidly.

"I did it again. I always mess up, don't I? I finally made it back to Luna, and what do I do? I say words that I know would hurt her feelings. I never take responsibility for anything I do or say. Everyone was right. I did hire that assassin. I did almost get everyone I loved killed. I didn't help Eve and Luna with their mission which started all of this in the first place. Luna met all those men because of my actions. I can't let it end like this. Luna was the one who was always alone. Now she has men who loves her. I should have been happy for her because I love her too. That's right… I love her too. I don't want to lose her again. I'm tired of making mistakes and hurting the ones I care about. I'm not giving up yet."

August stayed in the storming forest all night until the morning moon rose. Luna, along with her husbands, wakes to eat their morning meal when they hear a knock at the door.

Miquel frowns angrily. "I thought I told him to leave."

Cortez, curious about the situation, went with the feelings he was having. "Let's just see what he wants. He wouldn't have stayed in the storm all night if it wasn't important right?"

The five of them walk to the door an open it. August was standing soaked from the long-lasting storm. The thunder continues to crackle as the winds pick up.

Luna sees the weather was becoming dangerous. "August, get inside the storm is only getting worse. What are you still doing here anyway? My husband told you to leave."

August speaks softly to Luna as he understands her feelings. "Luna, I'm sorry. Please, I need to talk to you, all of you. If that's alright with you guys?"

Luna looks over to her men for approval. Miquel and the others nod their heads allowing August to explain himself to Luna. They were curious about what August had to say.

"I want to apologize. I'm aware that I've been an asshole to all of you. I know you guys see me as a brat since that's what you kept calling me. I never wanted to hurt any of you… especially you Luna. You sent your husbands to risk their lives to rescue me. I was barely hanging on in that cave I was in. If they hadn't built that home down there, I would have already been dead right now. Cortez, I'm sorry I screwed up your mission and almost got you killed. Luna would have never forgiven me if you would have died because I was afraid to carry on your orders."

"It's fine, I'm here now and that's what's important."

August smiles shyly. He knew Cortez may not have liked him in the beginning, but he sees how kind he truly is. "Yeah, that's true. Your husband Cortez isn't a bad guy, Luna. I just couldn't see how gifted these guys were because of my own feelings. You know, I was, and have always been, a little scared of everything. Even change. When I heard you had four husbands, I became jealous. Look at them, how can I even compete with these guys. Their strength and looks, plus they are the reason I made it out alive. You have every right to love whoever you wish, Luna. I take full responsibility for everything that has happened. I should have considered how you and Eve felt about your lives. I felt like I was losing a family. I didn't want to be alone."

Luna was confused by August last statement. "What do you mean August? You had your parents."

"Ha, my parents. I always knew you didn't like me because I've always bragged about them. It's time I told you the truth about my parents. My life has all been a lie."

"August what do you mean, a lie?"

"My parents were only as perfect and great as I made them sound. In reality my parents were horrible. My father would beat me every night till I bled. Sometimes he would even strike my mother. She didn't care about it, as long as she could live a life with money and useless items. I would starve for days because she didn't care to feed me. They hated that I was weak and wasn't very good at fighting and hunting. I would fail at everything my father wanted me to do. My mother blamed me for the reason my father beat her. She always told me that I was a waste of a child."

"Why didn't you tell Eve and me, August? We could have done something together to help you with your situation. We thought you were living a happy life this whole time."

"I wanted you and Eve to like me. I didn't want you to think I was a coward. Every day, I would cover my bruises and get heals from the village healer so you wouldn't notice my problems. The two of you have already been through enough. My problems wasn't important."

Luna takes on a sadden look. "Are you kidding me? Being beaten by your parents and starving is not right. That explains why you were always so hungry when you came over for dinner. I thought you were just being greedy. Everything I thought about you was a lie. You were protecting me and Eve's feelings."

"I was, and I'm sorry, Luna. I only wanted to enjoy our happy childhood together, not worry about my problems. That day you got angry at me when we were young really scared me. I didn't want to lose you as a friend. I had to do whatever it took to keep you happy for that day forward. You and Eve were the kindest friends anyone could ever ask for. I still manage to almost mess that up as an adult."

"I didn't see you as a coward years ago August. That day you saved me in the woods made me fall in love with you. I saw that you were willing to risk your life for me. That's why I invited you here. I will never forget how kind you were growing up together. After our fight as children, you were different in a good way. You always made me laugh and knew how to cheer me up. You just need to stop and think before you act for now on."

"Yeah, I realize that now from every time your husbands kicked my ass."

The men laugh at August comment.

"Look everyone, I don't want to pretend anymore that I'm brave or strong. I'm scared of people who are stronger than me and large creatures. This is who I am. I only acted the way I did so I could keep up a strong image in front of you guys. You guys are everything I wanted to be. Just do me a favor and keep loving Luna and keep her safe for me. You guys deserve her. I'll be leaving now."

"Wait, where are you going August? Back home?"

"No Luna, I was thinking about doing some traveling to find a place to live. The people of our old home platform hate me. Plus, my parents are still living there. My father even had the nerve to write how the King should have killed me on my burned down home. Oh well, right. That is all I wanted to say before I leave and start over. Goodbye Luna. Live a good life okay."

Luna stands there silently for a moment. Every thought came to her mind about their past. She never knew August had that type of painful life. She looks sadly over to her husbands. They roll their eyes and throw their hands up in submission. They knew what her look meant.

Miquel stops August before he walks out the door. He let out a sigh of annoyance before he spoke. "August wait. You can stay with us but only if you show who you truly are."

Marcel frowns but agrees to let August stay. "Yeah, no acting tough or we'll throw your ass out of here."

"What, really!? I can stay!"

Aaron folds his arms and scowls at August. "Don't get cocky August. You get one chance."

"Luna, are you alright with this decision?"

"Well, I don't know August. First, you have to pass my test for approval."

"I'll do anything you ask, just tell me what I have to do."

"Okay. First, you must say, Luna, you have the hottest, bravest, husbands ever."

August looks over in shock to her husbands who were all grinning at him.

Miquel covers his smile as he chuckles. "Go on August. Do what Luna ask."

August sighs as he prepares himself to repeat Luna's words. "Luna, you have the hottest and bravest husbands ever."

"Good, very good. Now say, I will respect them and the great sex they give you."

"Really Luna?" August says in a winey tone.

Luna's men laugh as they watch her torture August.

Cortez chuckles at Luna's actions. "Go on August, don't be shy."

"Fine." August says in a monotone voice. "I will respect them and the great sex they give you."

Luna's husbands claps as they laugh at August's pain.

Aaron was pleased to see the frown on August's face. It was good for them to have a fresh start. "Good job, August. You did well. I see you will do what needs to be done for Luna."

"Oh, he's not done yet."

"What do you mean Luna? I said what you wanted me to."

"Now I want you to kiss and suck my feet."

Everyone stops and stares at Luna in shock.

Cortez grins. "Miquel, I have plenty of leashes in the back if you need one."

"Yeah, I may have you grab one for me Cortez."

Marcel huffs as he looks at August. "Before you even think of doing that, let me heal your face. I'm tired of seeing your bloody bruises. You need to look good when you suck my wife's feet."

They all nod in agreement. Luna, on the other hand, was stunned by how handsome August had become after Marcel healed him. She almost forgot how attractive he was after not seeing him for years. She bit her lip as she truly studies August's body. His muscles and abs were more toned than from how she remembered him. Surviving in the blue crystal cave shaped August body in a way Luna couldn't ignore.

August feels appreciation from how Luna was looking at him. He gets down on one knee and begins to kiss and suck her toes. Luna let out a satisfying moan from the feeling.

"Hah, so good August. Now do the other one."

Cortez enjoys seeing Luna being pleased. "She is so naughty. Hah, I love her."

Her men smile and nod as they agree.

CHAPTER 36

NEW FAMILY

Time had passed since August moved in to live with the family. The other men had grown to like him once he started being himself. He would help Cortez with the farm and some chores around their home. The men promise to train August properly so he can defend himself and fight for Luna. As for Luna, she would often watch her husbands' training methods as they beat August senseless. She thought often that maybe they were beating him up for fun. She excuses the thought from her mind as they were taking the time to get familiar with him.

Cortez takes a break from their fun session of training. There was still one other important job for him to do around the farm. "Hey guys, I'll be back. I'm going to check on Blue and her egg. It should be ready to hatch soon."

Luna's expression changes to excitement. "Wonderful! I can't wait to see this new shadow creature!"

"Are we ready to raise a creature like that?"

Miquel shrugs his shoulders. "We have no choice, Aaron."

Everyone watches as Cortez comes running back with joy on his face. "Everyone, it's time! Blue's egg is about to hatch!"

They all run to the barn made for Blue to watch the new baby hatch. They can see a glimpse of shimmering dark blue fur as the hatchling emerges from the egg. The shadow owl bear was a beauty to look at. August prepares some warm towels so they can help clean the baby creature.

"Aww, it's so cute and fluffy. He's going to be huge. Are you sure you can handle another large creature Cortez?"

"Sure, I can Luna! These two will not be as big as my bird over there."

Luna's jaw drops when she sees Cortez pointing at a giant shadow eagle. The bird was twice the size as Blue.

"How did I not notice that thing this whole time living here?"

"Well Luna, most of the time my eagle's out finding food for my other creatures here. Every time you came out to the farm with me, he would be away somewhere."

"Did you tame him?"

"Nope Luna, I found his egg lost in the woods. I searched for his mother but when I found her, she had just been eaten by a shadow shark. It may have flown a little too low that day."

"Um, how big was this shark love?"

Cortez gently pats Luna's back. "You don't want to know, my love."

"Why am I so attracted to you right now? You are turning me on."

"Oh, really Luna? Want to solve that feeling later?"

"You bet I do."

August was seeing Luna flirt with Cortez and decides to go do something else. "I'll go get some more towels. Be back okay."

Miquel chuckles quietly. "Luna, are you still holding out on him?"

"Yep, I'm still punishing him for all the trouble he's cause."

"That must be torture. Sometimes you walk around the house naked. I would have broken down after seeing you like that."

Marcel laughs at the situation. "Yeah, I know Cortez, this is cruel what you are doing to him Luna. I can have to say that I find what you are doing entertaining."

Luna laughs at her men. "Fine, if you guys are standing up for him then he must have changed."

Aaron nods with agreement. "Yeah, he's finally being himself and doesn't act like a winey brat anymore. Even I find him fun to be around."

"Hmm, okay then, I will go see him tonight. I will go tell him to prepare for me."

Her men watch as Luna runs through the field to catch August.

"Hey guys, I bet August is going to come running to us for advice on how to handle Luna." Cortez says as he chuckles.

Aaron crosses his arms in doubt. "I doubt that would happen, Cortez."

"Okay then Aaron. Let's make a bet. If I win you have to cook dinner tonight and give me your night with Luna."

"Okay, I'll bet you. But if I win you have to give up your night with Luna and cook my favorite dish."

Miquel smiles at their silly bet. "This should be fun right Marcel?"

"Yep. We both know who's going to win."

They watch as Luna finally catches up to August in the field. "August, could you come here for a minute."

"Yes Luna, is something wrong?"

"Not at all. I was just wondering if I could come to your room tonight. I believe you've proved yourself to be mine."

"Wait, I can finally bond with you?"

"Yes, now be ready. I'm about to go take my bath now."

August looks nervous as Luna runs to the house. His nerves were getting the best of him. Luna's husbands see August run towards them with a nervous look on his face.

Aaron frowns at August. "No, don't you dare August!"

Aaron looks over to Cortez whose grin was so wide you can see all his teeth and fangs.

"Prepare to lose bro. We both know why he's running to us."

Marcel and Miquel laugh as they knew Cortez was correct. August was breathing heavy as he finally reached them.

"Guys, guys. I need some advice."

"Of course, you do August." Cortez says with a grin. "Go right on ahead and ask what you need."

Aaron continues to frown as Cortez grins.

"Guys, Luna finally wants to bond with me tonight. I don't know what to do. How did you guys prepare?"

Miquel was confused. "We didn't August. We went with our feelings and made love to her."

"What? No, I get that part. I feel the same for Luna but… how did you know what to do? You know, for as pleasing her body and stuff?"

Marcel chuckles. "We are just naturally gifted I guess."

The men laugh while August becomes even more nervous.

"Guys, this is serious. What if I mess up."

Miquel wraps his arm around August neck. "You will be fine August. Just relax, don't think so hard about it and just follow your feelings for her."

"Okay, thanks guys. I'm going to go prepare now."

As August run, Aaron becomes angry. "Damn. Now I have to give up one of my days with Luna and cook tonight."

Cortez gives him a slight punch in the arm. "Yeah, you do but you know what, we should go listen. You know, just to make sure everything goes well and stuff."

They all got the hint of what Cortez was implying.

Aaron grins at the idea. "Sure, I'm down."

"I'm pretty sure we are all thinking the same thing."

"Yeah Miquel, the fact that August is so going to screw up."

"That sounds about right Marcel. Let's go enjoy the show. I'm interested in what's going to take place."

CHAPTER 37

THE FINAL HUSBAND

Luna had dressed in her sexy pink transparent gown and was eager for August to see her. She makes her way to August room and softly knocks on it. She opens the door to see August in his robe and underclothes with his muscle tone chest exposed. She bites her lip as she sees how much work August has put into making his body strong. August slowly walks over to her and holds her close. He plants gentle kisses on her soft lips down to her neck.

He softly whispers in her ear. "Luna. You look so sexy right now."

"Really? How about you show me how much you love my sexiness."

August was becoming overly excited and tries to remember what the others had told him. He breathes slowly as he thinks.

"Just relax. The guys say just go with my feelings."

August takes another deep breath and starts to kiss and feel all over Luna's body. He squeezes her ass firmly while kissing and sucking her neck. August and Luna didn't realize the others were outside their room listening to them. Luna was busy enjoying the pleasing touch August was giving her.

"Hah, yes August. You are so gentle. I'm ready for you. It's been too long."

"Yes it has."

August slides down her panties and takes off her gown. He strips off his own and lays between her legs. Luna let out a moan as he slowly pushes his penis inside her. He begins to stroke slowly as he tries to control his emotions.

"Ah, August, yes. I can feel your... warmth? August! Did you just release in me already!?"

Luna and August symbol of bonding love forms on both their backs. Her men outside the door all look with surprise at one another. They place their hands over their mouths as they laugh silently.

"Luna, I'm so sorry. You felt so good I just…"

"We bonded in like 10 seconds August."

Her husbands run to one of the other rooms to hide as they hear Luna walking towards the door. She stumps out the door and slams it behind her. Augusts falls backwards onto the bed and covers his face.

"I really do suck, don't I?"

The next morning the others had set the table for their morning meal as they wait for Luna and August. August walks through the door seeing the men not giving him eye contact as they hold back their laugh. Luna walks in soon after slamming cups and dishes as she frowns angrily.

She grabs a plate of food and a drink so she can eat in the other room. She gives everyone but August a kiss before she walks out of the room.

The men were struggling at this point to keep from laughing.

"Go on and laugh guys. I know you heard what happen last night."

They all release their laugh as August speaks.

Aaron leans back in the chair holding his stomach from laughter, "Look August, we understand, really."

"No, you don't. I couldn't even last a minute. I never imagined she would feel that good. Do you guys realize how tight and wet she was?"

Miquel smiles as he sips his drink. He looks down at his cup as he thinks of Luna. "Yeah, we know all too well August."

"Luna hates me right now. I have to redeem myself guys."

"August now you know what to expect. Just prepare yourself mentally for when you try again. Try not to be intimidated by her."

"Yes, Cortez is right. Show her you're the boss. You have to own her August. I know I did back at my hideout. Such a naughty woman. I love it."

August takes Cortez and Marcel's words to heart. He places his head on the table and lets out a sigh of relief.

"Okay, thanks guys. I'm going to go try again."

They all cheer August on as he exits the door.

Cortez cheers him on. "You got this August!"

Aaron snickers. "He's going to fail."

Miquel grins at Aaron's comment. "There is a high possibility he will. What do you think Marcel?"

"I think we should listen again."

They grin mischievously and run toward where August and Luna would be.

August, seeing that Luna had finished her meal, goes to search the laundry area where she usually is after a morning meal. He spots her as she folds the clothes.

"Luna, can we talk?"

Luna pretends she doesn't hear him. Outside the door the others finally make it so they can hear what's about to happen.

"Luna, I know you hear me talking to you."

Luna, still ignoring him, tries to walk out the door when August grabs her by the arm. He pulls and pushes her up against the wall. He forcefully kisses and devours her lips causing her to moan. He begins stripping her clothes off as he continues to kiss her. August picks her up and lays her on the table. He slides inside her and aggressively pounds her.

"Hah, yes! Ah, yes! August this feels so much better. Don't' stop."

August thrust harder as he watches Luna's eyes roll from him pleasing her. He pulls her body off the table and bends her over. Luna tries to grip whatever she can find on the table as he pounds her from the back. Her moans satisfy August which makes him feel confident.

"Yes, August, yes!"

"You like how this feels Luna!?"

"Yes, this is so good!"

"Is it better than the others!?"

"No, it's not!"

Luna's husbands fall to the floor with laughter after hearing the conversation.

"Why would he ask that?"

Marcel holds his stomach as he laughs so hard. "I don't know Aaron but that was hilarious."

August stops what he was doing as he clearly hears the men laughing outside the door. "You know what, I think I hate those guys again."

***

The following morning Luna's husbands were out tending to the farm and the new baby shadow owl bear. August walks through the barn ready to help the men with their duties. They suddenly clap and cheer when they spot August. Cortez greets him as cheerful as always.

"Yayy, you did it August!"

Miquel chuckles slightly. "Yes, you manage to finish with in a respectable time."

August tries not to laugh as the men tease him. "You guys are real funny, you know."

They all give August a pat on the back as they play around.

Miquel was eager to give August the news. "August, we have good news for you. Luna is pregnant with you and Cortez's babies. Two little royal girls. Marcel and I figured out how to determine the sex of the baby before they are born. That's if anyone want to know the sex of their babies."

"Really! That's awesome news! I'm going to be the best father I can for my little girl. I must of did well last night to get her pregnant so soon."

"Not exactly, August. She got pregnant from the 10 seconds you gave her the day before. Cortez had sex with her the day before so that's how she's having the twins."

August face drops after hearing Miquel say his ten seconds got Luna pregnant. They all laugh and tease him once more.

"What name will you give your daughter August?"

"Let me think Cortez. How about I name her Anna."

Aaron nods with approval. "That's a pretty name. What about you Cortez? What will you name your daughter?"

"I was thinking, Cassie."

Marcel smiles at the name. "I like it. It fits well for your daughter."

"I hope we are all ready to have little Queens running around here."

Marcel agrees. "I'm ready Miquel. But there is no way our girls are going to be soft. They will train just like their brothers."

Cortez didn't mind having his daughters trained for fighting and defense. "Fair enough Marcel. Hey, let's all head back to the house. I have gifts I made for all of us."

They all joined Luna who was in the kitchen preparing their meal.

"Hey Luna, come over here I have something for you."

"Oh, what is it Cortez?"

"Ta da! Look, I made rings for all of us from the crystals I harvest back at the cave."

Luna gasps with excitement. "I love it, Cortez! It's so beautiful."

Miquel observes the rings. "They are nice Cortez. Thank you."

"You guys are always spoiling me, with gifts and love. How about all of you join me in the room for a little gift of my own. It's still early in my pregnancy, maybe we can have a little fun one last time before I rest."

Her husbands give a happy grin and follows her to the bedroom. Moments later they were making love to their beautiful wife.

"Ah Yes! Give me more! I want more of all of you!"

BONUS

"Hey Cyrus. We finally made it to this new platform."

"I know right, Miguel. I wonder what this world has to offer. I hope I can find some new undiscovered creatures."

"Yes, I hope I can find some new plants in herbs to help with my research. For now, we should lay low Cyrus. I heard some rumors about one of the Queens of this world."

"Yeah, I heard that too. Isn't she like, a whore or something?"

Before Miguel could answer a woman bumps into them as she was running. Her hood had fallen from her head revealing her long blue hair and glowing gentle purple eyes.

"I'm sorry guys." she says in a sweet gentle tone. "I must hurry!"

They watch as her hair blows in the wind like a wave in a large body of water. She runs quickly into the dark forest ahead.

"Who was that beauty?"

"I believe that was one of Queen Eve's daughters Cyrus."

"She's so beautiful." They both say.

Moments after the men see that she was being chased by royal guards.

"What the heck is going on around here Miguel? I have a bad feeling right now."

"Well, if that's the case then she may be in trouble. We need to help her Cyrus."

"I agree, let's get going bro."

ABOUT THE AUTHOR

Hey there readers. First, let me say thank you for taking the time to read Book Two. I really appreciate it. This one was really fun for me to write. I have always loved writing and creating stories. I usually get inspired by other books similar to my own. My favorite books have always been fantasy, books about out of this world creatures, and mythical beings. I like to separate myself from real life, I never like to write anything about our world today. You may notice my love for hot steamy scenes. This is something that I look for in other books I enjoy but often can't find it. So, I thought, well why not write it myself and put all the naughty things that I enjoy in my books. I not only write books but also enjoy the love of gaming. I grew up as a gamer girl and I still play games to this day. I Love those RPG games, puzzles, shooters, adventures games. You name it, I've probably played it. My last, but not least, passion is drawing. I have been drawing ever since I was a kid. You may notice I draw my own book covers and make art daily. It's something I do to clear my mind, now I use it to bring my characters to life. I hope you all stick around to enjoy the rest of my series for THE E.N.D'S TALE. I'm not done yet, so let's see how this series end. Again, thank you for all your support.

www.ingramcontent.com/pod-product-compliance
Lightning Source LLC
LaVergne TN
LVHW091043080826
845145LV00002B/601

* 9 7 8 1 9 6 0 7 5 9 0 3 0 *